D1187355

MOROCCAN
FOLKTALES

MIDDLE EAST LITERATURE IN TRANSLATION
Michael Beard *and* Adnan Haydar, *Series Editors*

Other titles in Middle East Literature in Translation

The Author and His Doubles: Essays on Classical Arabic Culture
   Abdelfattah Kilito; Michael Cooperson, trans.

The Committee
   Sonallah Ibrahim; Mary St. Germain and Charlene Constable, trans.

A Cup of Sin: Selected Poems
   Simin Behbahani; Farzaneh Milani and Kaveh Safa, trans.

Fatma: A Novel of Arabia
   Raja Alem with Tom McDonough

Fugitive Light: A Novel
   Mohammed Berrada; Issa J. Boullata, trans.

In Search of Walid Masoud: A Novel
   Jabra Ibrahim Jabra; Roger Allen and Adnan Haydar, trans.

Three Tales of Love and Death
   Out El Kouloub

Women Without Men: A Novella
   Shahrnush Parsipur; Kamran Talattof and Jocelyn Sharlet, trans.

Yasar Kemal on His Life and Art
   Eugene Lyons Hébert and Barry Tharaud, trans.

Zanouba: A Novel
   Out el Kouloub; Nayra Atiya, trans.

MOROCCAN
Folktales

Jilali El Koudia

Translated from the Arabic by Jilali El Koudia *and* Roger Allen
With Critical Analysis by Hasan M. El-Shamy

Syracuse University Press

First Edition 2003
03 04 05 06 07 08   6 5 4 3 2 1

Mohamad El-Hindi Books on Arab Culture and Islamic Civilization are published with
the assistance of a grant from Ahmad El-Hindi.

The paper used in this publication meets the minimum requirements of American
National Standard for Information Sciences—Permanence
of Paper for Printed Library Materials, ANSI Z39.48–1984.∞™

Library of Congress Cataloging-in-Publication Data

El Koudia, Jilali.
Moroccan folktales / Jilali El Koudia ; translated from the Arabic by
Jilali El Koudia and Roger Allen ; with critical analysis by Hasan M.
El-Shamy. — 1st ed.
p. cm. — (Middle East literature in translation) (Mohamad
El-Hindi Books on Arab Culture and Islamic Civilization)
Folktales gathered from members of the author's family.
Includes bibliographical references.
ISBN 0–8156–0789-X (alk. paper)
1. Tales—Morocco. I. El-Shamy, Hasan M., 1938– II. Title. III.
Series. IV. Series: Mohamed El-Hindi series on Arab culture and Islamic
civilization.
GR353.3 .E4 2003
398.2'0964—dc22   2003017915

Manufactured in the United States of America

Contents

Preface

IT HAS BECOME indisputable that folktales constitute an essential aspect of the culture of any country, a universal cultural heritage that calls for preservation. Because it is an oral tradition and depends on memory, it is in danger of perishing. Indeed, in the face of modern mass media, in particular audiovisual, these tales have been falling into neglect and oblivion. The parts they played in the past—entertainment, didactic, moral and religious instruction—are now being taken over by other mass media.

The teller of tales in marketplaces, in the *halqa* or circle, used to attract a large number of people who gathered to listen to stories of adventure—epic, romantic, fantastic, religious, and historic tales. The storyteller was usually a wandering traveler, gifted in this task and with a mission. The audience listened with great interest and memorized the stories and passed them on to other generations orally. This cultural heritage expressed the daily preoccupations of ordinary people from all kinds of social classes. It also reflects literary and artistic aspects of their society in general.

At home mothers and grandmothers were highly reputed as bearers of such treasure. In the absence of television, families used to gather around in the evenings to listen to such tales, their sole entertainment. Today, families sit in front of televisions, which have invaded almost all homes. Except for Jamaa Lafna in Marrakesh and a few marketplaces in the countryside or old towns where such tradition still struggles to survive, it is already becoming a part of the past.

The idea behind this book stems from an awareness of this situation and the intention to preserve such lore, in hopes that other similar attempts will follow. The urgent step to be taken is to collect some of these tales, the raw material itself, in order to make them available to future generations.

Born in a rural family, I used to listen to Mother telling us children some of these tales, the only means of entertainment and relief from daily hardships. Mother is then my first source of most of these stories. In recent years I have asked her to retell them, and I took notes and then rebuilt them and translated them into English. The same procedure was followed with other women, particularly older ones. Such stories are collected from various regions of Morocco such as Tetuan, Al-Huceima, Taza, Fes, Marrakesh, and Tahanout.

Most of the time my narrators told the same stories but in different versions, so I had to make a selection, discarding repetitions. In fact, the work I have done is more of rewriting, reconstructing the plots, and filling the gaps than just translation. This is because most of my narrators were wordy, repetitive, and kept going back and forth trying to recall the stories from memory.

The final version was submitted to Professor Roger Allen, who expressed his deep interest in such work and kindly offered to revise the language and style. The alterations he has introduced have made the stories readable and intelligible to an English-speaking audience.

Acknowledgments

I AM DEEPLY GRATEFUL to Professor Roger Allen for his moral support and his tremendous contribution.

Professor Allen and I would like to express our thanks to Professor Hasan El-Shamy for writing the afterword and providing the categorization of the folktales, and to Professors Deborah Kapchan and Dan Ben-Amos for their assistance in bringing this project to fruition.

My sincere thanks are also due to my narrators, in particular my mother, Tahra; my sister, Sofia; my wife, Mehdia; her mother, Hadja Oum Keltoum, Rokia; my niece, Nadia; my student Belaali Chakir; Amina Ait Belarbi; and Malika and her women friends.

May 2003   Jilali El Koudia

Jilali El Koudia is a professor of English and comparative literature at the University of Fez in Morocco. He is the author of several short stories and has also compiled a collection of Moroccan short stories in English translation. He gathered these folktales from several of the women in his family.

Roger Allen is a professor of Arabic language and literature at the University of Pennsylvania. His books include *The Arabic Novel: An Historical and Critical Introduction, Second Edition*, and a cotranslation of *In Search of Walid Masoud* by Jabra Ihrahim Jabra, both published by Syracuse University Press.

Hasan M. El-Shamy is a professor in the Department of Folklore and Ethnomusicology at Indiana University. He is the author of *Folk Traditions of the Arab World: A Guide to Motif Classification* (1995) and *Types of the Folktale in the Arab World: A Demographically-Oriented Tale-Type Index* (forthcoming).

MOROCCAN
FOLKTALES

Seven Brothers and a Sister

[1]

LONG, LONG AGO there was a family with eight children, seven sons and one daughter, named Aisha. She was the youngest and most cherished child in the family. One day her father and mother drowned in the flooding river while trying to save a cow. Afterward, her brothers took care of her and provided her with everything she needed. They rebuilt the house in case something happened to her during their absence and put locks on seven doors. Whenever they went out hunting or working on the land, they avoided any risks by firmly locking all the doors. With time she got bored and lonely, but they soon found her a beautiful cat to keep her company.

She named it Minoush. Almost immediately they took to each other and became the best of friends. To seal their friendship they swore to share everything and never betray one another. The brothers were very happy to see their sister and the cat on such good terms. Aisha no longer complained of boredom or loneliness, even when her brothers were out the whole day. They felt sure she was safe with the cat there, but they still locked all seven doors behind them whenever they went out.

One day they decided to travel far away on business. They took every possible precaution to leave their sister in a safe house. They brought her all the provisions she would need during their long absence so that she would not need to go out. Early one morning they woke up, embraced her fondly, and said farewell both to her and to her companion. Then they locked the seven doors and departed.

Days passed, and Aisha and Minoush were happy together, talking and playing. Aisha cleaned the house and prepared the meals that she shared with the cat. Everything was going perfectly well until Aisha came across a chickpea while sweeping the floor. The cat was resting in bed. Aisha picked the chickpea off the floor and wiped it on her dress. Minoush raised her head and asked for her share, but Aisha was greedy and ate it all.

The cat was angry and went off in a huff, but, even so, she kept quiet and pretended to go to sleep. Later in the day, while Aisha was busy kneading flour to make bread, the cat slipped into the kitchen, pissed on the box of matches, then went back to sleep.

When night fell and it started getting cold, Aisha went into the kitchen to make the fire and heat the food. But, much to her disappointment, she discovered that the matches were soaking wet.

"Oh, Minoush," she said, turning to the cat, "the matches are wet. What can we do?"

The cat acted surprised. "Well," she replied, "why don't you go out and borrow some matches from a neighbor?"

Aisha had no choice. So she opened the seven doors and for the first time went outside. In the dark night she spotted a fire glowing somewhere that seemed not too far away. She kept walking for a long time until she reached a hut. As she approached the door, it opened as if of its own accord. Suddenly, her eyes fell on an old ghoul. His eyes were flashing at her like twin embers. For a chair he was using a donkey's head, and for a turban he had a donkey's intestines wrapped around his head. He kept stirring a large black pot with a donkey's leg. At the very sight of him Aisha froze to the spot in panic, and her tongue stuck to her palate.

The ghoul stared straight at her. "What do you want?" he demanded in a disgruntled tone.

When she could not reply, he repeated his question with more menace.

She started shaking all over. "I need fire, Uncle Ghoul," she managed to say after great effort.

"Oh, so that's what you've come for. Certainly you can have some."

With that he selected a few embers, laid them on a zinc plate, and handed it to her. As she came close, he scratched her soft arm with his sharp claws as though by accident. She whispered her thanks and started walking home; blood was dripping from her arm all the way.

After a while, the ghoul went out and sniffed the ground. He followed the scent of blood until he found where Aisha was living. He knocked on the door and waited, licking his lips. Aisha was still shaking with fear when she heard the knock. She imagined her brothers had returned and took heart.

"Who is it?" she asked.

"O Aisha, dear heart," he intoned in his resounding voice, "open the door for me."

She felt numb and did not open the door.

"Tell me," he asked her after a long pause, "how did you find me sitting?"

"O Uncle Ghoul, you were sitting on a chair of gold."

"What did you see on my head?"

"A silk turban."

"And what was I doing?"

"Stirring soup."

"With what?"

"With a silver spoon."

The ghoul was flattered. He only knocked the first door down, then went away satisfied.

Thus, every night at the same hour he came back and asked her the same questions. Aisha gave him the same answers, and he broke one door every night.

On the seventh day she found herself in real trouble; she was beside herself with worry because there was only one door left to separate her from the ghoul. When night fell, his visiting hour was drawing near. Her fear intensified with every passing minute; her heart kept beating faster and faster, its thumping like the drum of fate. She found no consolation in the cat, which simply remained silent and sat resting in a corner and watching her with shining eyes. Aisha wished her brothers had never gone away and blamed them for what was happening to her. She wrapped herself in a thick cloth and curled up in a corner, trembling with fear, hunger, and cold. Finally, she gave up all hope and yielded herself to her imminent demise. When she heard stumbling footsteps, her heart almost stopped beating. She tried holding her breath to listen carefully, but her heartbeats deafened her ears. What was written was written, and she could do nothing to alter her fate.

Suddenly, her ears distinguished many voices outside; to her, they sounded like her brothers' voices. Her heart began to beat with a different rhythm. Or was it just her imagination? She took off the cover and stood close to the door listening. She could clearly make out her brothers talking among themselves, expressing their shock at the discovery of the six broken doors.

They had just returned from their journey after a long absence. They knocked cautiously on the door, not knowing what they would find. Aisha rushed to open it. Overwhelmed with joy at seeing them, she fell in their arms crying. They, too, were extremely delighted that she was still alive. When she remembered that it was almost time for the ghoul's visit, she started thinking fast. She locked the door and told her brothers what had happened. In just a matter of minutes the ghoul would be there to eat them all. She wasted no time on details. The seven brothers moved fast. They immediately dug a large hole beneath the door, covered it with hay and stood inside, waiting silently. Aisha stood glowing among her seven brothers, enjoying their protection.

At that moment the ghoul arrived and knocked at the last door. When she did not open it, he asked her as usual, "O Aisha, dear heart, what was I sitting on?"

"A donkey's head," she now replied in a defiant tone.

"What was on my head?"

"A turban made from a donkey's bowels."

"And what was I doing?"

"Stirring rotten water."

"With what?"

"With a donkey's leg."

With each answer the ghoul became more angry, and with the last one his wrath reached its climax. Taking a step back, he charged forward with all his might. The door flew open, and he fell right into the hole. Instantly, the seven brothers dumped firewood over him and set the fire. They gathered around the hole to watch him burn to ashes. Aisha stood over him, watching with pride and triumph.

As the ghoul was dying, he stuck his arm out from the middle of embers and shook his hand toward Aisha. "Remember, Aisha," he yelled, "you shall die at my hands!"

When the flames swallowed him, she simply gave a mocking laugh.

One day several years later, when the ghoul was almost completely forgotten, Aisha was sitting on the roof of the house watching her brothers at work in the nearby field. That very day Minoush had died of old age, but Aisha did not mourn her; the cat was always in a bad mood and withdrawn within herself. Aisha was greasing her hair with olive oil and combing it. As she was singing to herself, a shadow came between her and the sun. Looking up, she saw a raven. He hovered around her, then landed on the ground and started searching for food. He went on digging with his beak and claws until he reached the spot where the ghoul had burned to death and was buried. The black bird fished for a bone, then picked it up in his beak and flew over her head. Suddenly, the bone slipped from the raven's beak and fell on her, piercing her head like an arrow. She dropped dead on the spot.

The Pigeon Hunter

[2]

ONCE UPON A TIME there lived a man who had two wives. The first one was childless, but the second gave him a daughter and then got pregnant again. Every day he went up into the mountains to catch pigeons. He used to catch just two pigeons and give them to each of his wives alternately to prepare a meal. One day it was the second wife's turn to receive the pigeons. While she went to the kitchen to fetch a knife, she gave the birds to her daughter to hold. The pigeons started wildly flapping their wings, which scared the girl; they slipped out of her grasp and flew away. She shouted to her mother, who came running, but the pigeons had already perched on a tree, enjoying their newly gained freedom.

Mother and daughter now had to try to retrieve them. The mother spotted a herdsman. She begged him to help her and promised in return to give him one. The herdsman made tremendous efforts and managed to catch them, whereupon he gave them to the mother. But when he reminded her of her promise, she ignored him and started walking back home. Feeling very angry, the herdsman kicked her arm. Once again the pigeons escaped. This time they flew very far, and the mother and daughter had to chase them on their own. They went farther and farther away until they found themselves in a thick forest.

When they were deep in the forest and had been walking for a long time, the daughter started feeling tired. She begged her mother to stop for a rest. But the mother's eyes were riveted upon the two pigeons as they lured her farther and farther from home. After some time the daughter looked around and saw a dog. She called out to her mother, "Look, Mama!" she said. "My uncle's dog is following us. He wants to show us the way back home."

But the mother kept walking ahead, her eyes still fixed on the pigeons. After a while the daughter looked back again and saw a cat following in their footsteps. "Look!" she yelled. "Uncle's cat is just behind us. He wants to guide us back home."

But still the mother paid no attention and drudged on. By now, she was sweating all over; her eyes ached, and her legs felt as if they were falling off. When the daughter could drag her feet no longer, she looked around and saw a donkey. She was very happy. "Mama," she shouted to her mother, "there's Uncle's donkey. He wants to carry us back home."

Finally, when the mother ran out of energy and could see nothing in the impenetrable darkness of the forest, she stopped and turned around. It was then that she saw something that drained all her remaining energy. She could not even talk, but just whispered. "Oh, my dear daughter!" she said. "That's no donkey! That's a lion, and it'll eat us up! Run!"

They took refuge under a big oak tree. The mother was so heavy with the baby in her womb that she could not climb the tree. She sat down and spoke to her daughter. "Climb the tree, daughter," she urged. "If you see the lion starting to eat me on the right side, make some leaves fall to cover up the baby, since it'll be a boy. But if he starts on the left side, it'll be only another daughter."

Just at that moment the lion arrived, and the daughter shinned up the tree. The hungry animal immediately planted its teeth in the mother's right side. Her daughter started working fast with her fingers, making leaves fall like a shower. The baby was completely covered under a pile of leaves, and the lion did not notice him. When it had finished eating the mother, it started shaking the tree to bring the daughter down, but the tree was too solid for the animal. So, it lay down, waiting for her to get tired and come down.

Suddenly, a crow arrived and landed on a branch right in front of the weeping daughter. "I'll save you," the crow said, "if you'll promise to give me half of your mother's garments to furnish my nest."

The girl agreed, and the crow flew away and disappeared for a while. Before long he returned, carrying a red-hot plowshare. He addressed the lion. "Uncle Lion," he said, "you're still hungry. If you open your mouth all the way to your ears I'll jump into it."

When the lion had opened its mouth wide, the crow dropped the plowshare in and then gouged out its eyes. The daughter was now able to climb down safely. She gave the crow half the garments, wrapped up her baby brother in the other half, and went on her way.

She traveled through the jungle, carefully cradling her brother in her arms. From time to time she gave him a drop of water to keep him alive. When she came upon a she-wolf in labor, she stopped to watch. Realizing that the wolf was in trouble, the girl took pity, put her baby brother on the grass, and went over to help the wolf deliver her cubs. The she-wolf was so grateful to her that, as a reward for her assistance, she invited her to bring her baby brother to suck milk from her teats. She then offered her one of the cubs to take with her as a gift. So the sister took both babies and went happily on her way.

Another day she came across a tigress in labor, and again she gave help. The tigress gave her baby brother some milk and offered her a cub. The sister made a large reed basket, filled it with dry grass, and used it to carry her brother and the other babies. Then she found a she-monkey trying to deliver her babies, and again she helped and earned the same reward as before. And when she met a lioness in labor, she added one more baby to her basket. Then it was a she-bear, a leopard, and finally a hedgehog. Her baby brother, having drunk milk from all seven female animals, now looked very healthy and started to smile.

The sister collected all seven baby animals and cared for them in the same way as she did her brother. She fed them on whatever she found to eat in the jungle and gave them enough water. Before long the baby animals started providing for themselves and were growing up fast. Meanwhile, her brother was growing more slowly and was still very dependent on her. Although he looked small, he was wily and full of activity. The seven animals played with him all the time and guarded him from snakes and other dangers.

One day the sister had an idea. She climbed to the top of a mountain and sat down with her brother in her lap. The other animals gathered around her in a circle and waited. She closed her eyes and raised her arms toward the sky; the animals raised their paws as well, following her lead. There was a moment of absolute silence. Then the sister started praying to God, tears streaming from her eyes: "Oh, my God, please hear my prayer. Make my brother a grown-up man." The animals echoed her in chorus. When she opened her eyes again, her brother was no longer in her lap. She looked around and saw a strong young man sitting on the back of a white horse and well armed. The beasts bowed to him and greeted him warmly. The young man lifted his sister up behind him and rode away. Wherever he went, the animals followed him.

Thus, they traveled farther and farther, until they found themselves in a desert where there was neither food nor water. Night fell, and they gathered to rest. While the young man was discussing what to do next with his sister, a ghoul suddenly appeared out of the blue.

The ghoul greeted them and addressed the young man who was sitting in the center. "You are welcome here," he said. "I have a large dwelling and enough food and water for all of you. Why don't you come with me?"

The young man welcomed the invitation, and they all followed the ghoul to his home.

The ghoul was indeed extremely hospitable and had ample

food and water. They all ate and drank their fill and slept comfortably the whole night. In the morning the host enjoyed their company and invited them to stay as long as they wished. They were very happy and stayed for a long time. As day followed day, the ghoul and the young man became intimate friends and were always seen together. They swore never to betray or forsake each other.

One day the young man was riding his horse as he explored the neighborhood. He came close to an oasis where some Bedouins had settled with their camels. There he met a shepherdess who was as beautiful as a pearl and fell in love with her. He decided to visit her family and ask for her hand. When he returned home, he broke the news to his sister. She was very jealous and argued with him. He ignored her objection, as he was head over heels in love with the beautiful girl.

When his sister happened to be alone with the ghoul, she addressed him in honeyed tones and asked him to kill her brother.

The ghoul was surprised. "How can I do that?" the ghoul asked. "We have sworn fidelity to one another. I cannot do it."

But she kept tempting him. "If you kill him," she said eventually, "I'll marry you and be faithful to you forever."

Finally, the ghoul agreed to her proposal.

The following day the young man and the ghoul were ready to go out hunting as usual.

"Let's not take the beasts today," the ghoul suggested. "They need a rest."

Not suspecting anything, the young man consented, and they departed.

After they had left, the sister started grinding grain on the millstone. She was singing a sweet song, and the beasts, attracted by her voice, all gathered around and fell asleep.

When the young man and the ghoul reached a marsh, the ghoul stood in front of the horse and told its rider, "Get off the horse. I'm very sorry, my friend, but I have to eat you."

The young man was shocked and reminded him of their

pledge. However, the ghoul was now showing him an entirely different face, and the young man realized that he really meant what he said.

"All right," he replied after a moment's reflection. "If this is to be my fate, please allow me to say three words before you eat me."

"You're allowed even seven if you like," the ghoul replied.

The young man called out the seven names of his animals and was on the point of getting off his horse.

Meanwhile, back in the house the seven beasts were fast asleep. The sister was singing softly and grinding the grain. The hedgehog was sleeping just under her elbow. Suddenly, he stirred and knocked the millstone, which made its ax strike her right in the eye. Immediately, she went blind. The hedgehog woke his companions and warned them that the young man was in danger. He urged them to speed to his rescue. They all jumped up and followed his scent.

In no time they were at the marsh. They saw their friend getting off the horse and about to be eaten by the ghoul. The animals formed a circle around them. The young man gave them a gesture, and in less than a second they had torn the ghoul into tiny pieces. They collected his bones and buried them at the edge of the marsh.

The young man caressed them all and gave them a pat on the head. He rode back home surrounded by his animals. He found his sister still crying and asked her what had happened. She complained to him that the hedgehog had struck her while she was grinding grain for his animals. He comforted her and said such a thing would never happen again. As soon as she calmed down, she asked him about the ghoul. He told her he had killed and buried him in the marsh. She insisted that he show her where he was buried, so he took her to the spot.

A few days later, the young man met the Bedouin girl again and arranged for the wedding ceremony. The sister no longer protested and kept very quiet. On the wedding night she sneaked out to the marsh and collected seven bones from the ghoul's remains. Without being noticed she stuffed the bones in her brother's bed and went to sleep, pretending she was ill.

Later in the night, when the ceremony was over, the bride and groom were led to their bedroom. As the young man lay down on his bed to relax, the seven bones went straight into his body; there he lay dead still. Seeing him in that state, the bride assumed he was exhausted and fell asleep beside him. Next morning the girl shook him, but he remained motionless. She informed her family, and they discovered he was dead. Since it was very hot, they immediately took him to a graveyard and buried him. Thus, the wedding was turned into a funeral.

On the third day after his burial, in accordance with tradition, mourning was declared over. Everyone made ready to depart. The Bedouin chieftain gathered his men together and discussed what to do with the animals the young man had left behind. They agreed that they were savage and would be a danger both to them and to their cattle. So, the chieftain ordered his people to shut themselves inside their tents and huts. He then set the animals free so they could go back to the wild life where they belonged.

All eyes inside the tents and huts were glued to holes and openings in order to watch the beasts go free.

The seven animals walked slowly out and congregated in front of the door. They seemed to sniff each other as if debating among themselves what to do. People were fascinated by such a sight and stayed just where they stood in order to have a clear view of their next move. The animals started walking in file and in an orderly fashion, the lion leading the way. They walked toward the graveyard. The Bedouins assumed that since the animals had not eaten for three days, they were going to open the grave and devour the corpse.

As soon as they entered the graveyard, the animals started sniffing the graves until they stood over a fresh one. Then they began to scratch and dig with their claws until they had retrieved the entire corpse. They unwrapped the white shroud, so the young man emerged completely naked. People looked on breathlessly, eyes popping. Inch by inch the animals probed the body with their tongues and claws. From close up people could see them removing sharp bones and throwing them away one by one. When the hedgehog finally pulled out the seventh and last bone, the young man revived. His hands went straight to cover his groin. "Quick, bring me my burnous!" he shouted.

The Bedouins could not believe what they had just seen and remained nailed to the spot. The chieftain rushed to the house and brought the burnous and the horse. Afraid to come any closer to the animals, he threw the burnous over the young man and waited. The young man covered himself and jumped on his horse and rode home with his companions behind him.

The chieftain, who was also the father of the bride, ordered his people to collect the seven bones. He gave them to an old woman who was famous for her magic powers. After examining them for a while, she declared that they belonged to a ghoul. The Bedouins discussed the matter at length and found the culprit. They brought her out to be judged in public. The chieftain then asked his people to dig a deep hole, and there they buried the seven bones along with the young man's sister.

Thereafter, the wedding party was renewed with yet more jubilation and enthusiasm. The young man married the girl he was in love with, and they both lived happily ever after.

The Sultan's Daughter

[3]

LONG, LONG AGO there lived a sultan who was well respected by his people. God had endowed him with three daughters, but he had no son. The youngest daughter was the most beautiful and was her father's favorite. All her requests were promptly granted. Naturally, her sisters became very jealous of her and started making her life hard. And so, in order to live in peace with them, she asked her father to build her a palace of her own and to provide her with servants. Once her wish had been fulfilled, she allowed no one to approach her palace, having made up her mind to live as a hermit.

In the neighboring country, the son of another powerful sultan heard the story of the beautiful damsel living alone in her palace. He sent her a message, but she ignored it. He started frequenting her palace and managed to make clear his desire to marry her. She accepted, but only with many conditions. He had to provide her with one hundred of everything she asked for. When he had fulfilled all the conditions, she still did not allow him to make public visits to see her; instead, he had to dig a tunnel under her palace and visit her only during mealtimes. All this was not impossible for a sultan's son, especially since he was so in love with her. Thus, their meetings became more regular.

Despite the total secrecy, rumors of what was happening reached her sisters' ears. Their curiosity was roused: how did the young man look, and why did he come through a secret tunnel? They begged their father and then sent their sister a message, saying how very much they had missed her and how they longed to see her. At these words her heart melted, and she believed that their jealousy was a thing of the past. So she forgave them and allowed them to pay her a visit.

After agreeing on a plan they went to see her. They suggested taking her to the *hammam*, the public bath, and she liked the idea. Once there, they pretended they had forgotten something. Leaving her with the servants, they hurried back to her room to get a glimpse of the young man. They had made their precise calculations to coincide with his visit. Upon investigation they discovered that the tunnel was made of glass. When they heard him making his way through the tunnel, they started throwing stones. A sharp piece of broken glass went straight into his eye and did him a serious injury. Furious at what had happened, he retreated in agony.

The sisters quickly rejoined their sister at the bath and helped her wash. She thanked them and returned home, assuming that her visitor would be waiting for her. But he was not there. She waited for a long time. When he did not show up, she began to suspect that something had happened to him. She went into the tunnel to see if he had left her a message, and there she found pieces of broken glass and drops of blood. For just a moment she paused for thought, and then it dawned upon her that her sisters had conspired against her during their brief absence from the bath. She realized that, unfortunately, neither time nor distance can cure jealousy.

Leaving the palace she found an old beggar woman who always sat around the corner. She invited the woman in and talked to her in her private room. After exchanging clothes, she left her palace and went in search of her future husband disguised in dirty, tattered garments.

During the day she walked a few miles, and at night she lay down to sleep under a willow tree. Two pigeons took refuge for the night in the same tree. Perching just above her head they started talking about two lovers and how the sisters of the young woman had interfered to destroy their relationship. They said the young man was in grave danger of losing his sight forever. The two pigeons concluded their night talk by saying that the only cure for the young man was the ash of their feathers.

The two pigeons fell sound asleep. She meanwhile climbed the tree and caught them. Then she proceeded to pluck most of their feathers, burn them, and collect the ash in a piece of cloth. Next morning she continued her search for her lover's palace. Taking her for a beggar or madwoman, the palace guards stopped her at the entrance, but she insisted on seeing the sultan, saying she was bringing him an urgent message. When she told them that she had the cure for his son, she managed to convince them. A messenger was sent to tell the sultan about the mission of an old woman. He immediately received her.

In the sultan's presence, she cleaned his son's eyes with warm water, then sprinkled a few pinches of the ash on them. She advised him to keep them shut for at least an hour. When the sultan offered her a reward, she declined, saying that it was a cure from God.

She returned hurriedly to her palace and entered, still in disguise. She thanked the old woman and gave her plenty of gold and silver. Once the old beggar had left, the young woman ordered her cook to make a special cake that looked exactly like her. Then she laid her replica in bed and covered it in a clean white sheet, leaving only the face uncovered.

After about two hours the sultan's son opened his eyes. He was feeling no pain whatsoever, and had completely regained his sight. Overjoyed, he asked to see the old woman who had cured him, but he was told she had already left. Taking his sword he jumped on his horse and went in search of the girl who he thought had betrayed him. He was determined to take his revenge.

When he arrived at the palace, he entered secretly through the tunnel and headed straight for her bedroom on tiptoe. There he saw her, lying comfortably in her bed and smiling as she slept. "Oh, what cruelty can lurk beneath such beauty!" he thought to himself. Unsheathing his sword, he chopped off her head. When a piece of pastry popped into his mouth, he realized he had been deceived once more. He stood on guard and looked around, but everything was quiet and all the doors were locked. As he bent over to uncover the false woman, suddenly someone jumped on his neck and started kissing him. Then she told him what her sisters had done to her and how she had come by the cure for his injuries. When he learned the whole truth, he fell tearfully into her arms. And they lived together in complete happiness ever after.

The Fisherman

[4]

RIGHT AT THE EDGE of the town there stood a shabby hut, not far from a large river. Everyone knew it belonged to a very poor fisherman whose only source of living was whatever fish he managed to catch. There he lived with an ailing wife and a young daughter. As day followed day his wife's health went from bad to worse. When she felt her day had come, she collected whatever jewels she had inherited from her ancestors and locked them in a *hijan*, a very special box. She placed it on a window and whispered to it: "Please, promise never to be removed from your spot except at the hands of my own daughter." The *hijan* gave its promise. Then she called out to her husband and confided to him what she had done. She asked him not to remarry until their daughter had grown up. With the baby in his arms and tears in his eyes, he gave his promise. That very night the mother died quietly and peacefully in her bed.

The only surviving relative of the late mother was a widowed sister who had a blind daughter of her own. When her sister died, she felt sorry for her niece and started visiting her regularly. She was very kind to her and treated her like her daughter. As the niece grew up a little, her aunt started coaxing her to persuade her father to marry her. But when the daughter spoke to her father about it, he refused; he explained to her that he had given her mother his word not to marry while she was still a child.

The aunt continued to show great affection and kindness to the niece until the latter revealed to her the secret of the *hijan*. One day her aunt lifted her up to the window until her small hands could touch the box. Out it came. That day the aunt dressed her up like a grown-up girl. When the father came home, he noticed that the *hijan* had been removed from its place. He was feeling in a good mood, so this time, when his daughter asked him again to marry her aunt, he accepted. Next day the aunt moved in with her furniture and blind daughter.

Once the aunt had settled in, her attitude toward her niece began to change. She made the girl's life unbearable and treated her like a slave. Every day she sent the girl down to the river to clean the fish her father had caught. The niece felt more and more miserable, but she kept her tears concealed from her father.

One day he brought home three fish and gave them to his wife to prepare for lunch. When he went out again, she sent the niece to the river as usual. The girl took the knife and was on the point of cutting off a fish's head when it looked up into her eyes and spoke. "Please, please, don't kill me," it begged. "Throw me back into the river. I want to live."

"I can't," she said as she started to cry. "My aunt will give me a severe beating."

The fish felt sorry for her. "Now," it said, "listen to me carefully! Don't be afraid of that woman. She will beat you six times, and I will take them all. On the seventh you'll scream, and she'll bury you in a deep hole. But there's nothing to be afraid of; you'll find me there waiting for you with a nice surprise."

The girl let the fish slip from her hand. For a short while it disappeared, then it emerged as a mermaid and dived once more into the deep waters. The girl cut and cleaned the remaining two fish, put them in her basket, and went home. Her aunt counted the fish and found one missing. She was furious and scolded her. "Where's the third fish?" she asked. "To whom did you give it?" The girl sat down without saying a word. When she did not reply, her aunt brought a stick and started beating her hard. Six strokes and still the girl felt nothing. On the seventh her aunt raised the stick higher and whipped her with all her might. A sharp scream was heard that deafened her aunt. Seizing her niece by the hair, she dragged her to a long-neglected *metmoura*, or deep hole, inhabited only by black scorpions and snakes. She opened it, lowered her niece down, and then shut the cover.

The woman looked for a mortar, or *mehras*, and dressed it up like a girl. She laid it down on the bed and put a cover over it. When the father came for lunch, his daughter failed to greet him at the door as usual. That made him sad. "Where is my daughter?" he asked his wife.

She hesitated, answering first that she was out visiting some neighbors, then saying she was asleep. He went to her bed and tried to shake her awake, but she remained immobile. He took off the cover and, to his horror, found only the copper mortar. Realizing then that something had happened to his daughter at the hands of her wicked aunt, he tied the latter to a post in the middle of the courtyard and started whipping her with a rope. On the seventh stroke she confessed her evil deed and showed him where she had buried her niece alive.

The father rushed to the *metmoura*. When he opened it, he saw something he had never witnessed in his life before. Everything gleamed with gold and silver, and his daughter was seated in comfort on an ivory throne. She was a princess dressed in the finest of clothes and wearing mother-of-pearl. For a long time he just stood above her in fascination, but then he managed to ask her to climb up and join him. However, she told him she could not and narrated to him the story of the mermaid.

From then on he used to open up the hole every single day and beg her to come up, but in vain. He could neither reach her, nor could she climb up to him. Day by day, he sat beside the *metmoura*, his heart melting in anguish. The daughter, too, shed tears in torrents as she waited for the mermaid to give her permission to leave.

Seeing the father becoming more and more miserable and the daughter's distress, the mermaid pitied them and at last released her. She gave her all the treasures to take up with her. But the mermaid advised her never to trust her aunt and warned her that someday the wicked woman would take her revenge.

The father gave his daughter a separate room where no one could see her. There she settled amid the treasures that the mermaid had offered her. The aunt was absolutely forbidden to come any closer to her. The daughter led a quiet and peaceful life. And so it was that the mermaid paid her a visit every day, bringing her everything she desired.

Meanwhile, the father continued to lead his normal life, fishing in the river in order to feed his wife and her blind daughter. It was still the same shabby hut set apart from the other dwellings. The aunt now seemed quite obedient and silent.

One day the sultan decided to find a wife for his son and heir. He sent a messenger to invite people to the wedding ceremony. The fisherman was out at the river when the messenger came to his door to invite the whole family. When the aunt went to answer the door, her niece stood by the window to listen. Once the messenger had left, she looked out of the window and asked her aunt if she too could attend the festivities. Her aunt refused.

As night fell, the party began. A forest of candles illuminated the area around the palace. Music filled the air and could be heard everywhere. The niece was amazed by the sound and could not resist. The house was very quiet; even her father had gone. So she dressed up and sneaked out of her room. Like a fox she walked until she reached the palace wall, and then climbed up to the roof where she had a good view. There she sat to enjoy the whole scene.

At around midnight the party was coming to an end, and people started going back home. The girl hurried home before her aunt and father arrived. One of her slippers slipped off her foot and fell in the sultan's courtyard where the horses were standing.

Next morning one of the sultan's slaves found the slipper. It was so beautiful that he assumed it could belong only to a princess. He took it to the sultan and showed it to him. But the sultan had never seen a slipper like it. He sent for an old woman and asked her to search every house for the owner of that slipper. The old woman did the rounds from door to door showing the slipper. Whenever women set eyes on it, they exclaimed, "What a slipper!"

After a prolonged search, the woman returned to the sultan. "I am sorry, my lord," she said, "but no one claims this slipper."

But he insisted: "Have you looked everywhere?"

She hesitated for a second, remembering that she had neglected the fisherman's hut. Actually, she was convinced it would be impossible for such a wonder to be found in that shabby hut.

The sultan commanded her to check even there. "We never know," he said. "What can be found in the river may not be found in the sea."

Without much hope the old woman walked toward the fisherman's hut. When she knocked at the door, the aunt opened it. She showed the aunt the slipper, and once more the aunt, just like all the previous women, simply exclaimed, "What a slipper!"

Just at that moment the niece was standing at the window and saw the woman still holding the slipper. "Oh, my slipper!" she shouted. "Give me back my slipper!"

The old woman looked up in surprise, but, just to make sure, she said, "Show me the second."

The girl flashed it in her direction. Immediately, the old woman turned around and rushed back to tell the sultan the good news.

The sultan gathered his family and dignitaries and discussed the matter with them. Later, the sultan, his son, and a few dignitaries were to be seen dragging a fat bull and walking in the direction of the fisherman's hut. At the door of the lowly hut the sultan slew the bull. Just then the fisherman arrived from the river and stood there stunned by the whole scene. The sultan greeted him with a great respect that made him tremble. He stood there still holding the basket of fish and not knowing what to do or say. Then the sultan explained to him the purpose of his visit. The fisherman was both flattered and astonished. "How can a poor man such as myself be the future father-in-law of the sultan?!" he pondered.

The basket of fish fell from his hand, and he went in to break the news to his daughter. Her face glowed with happiness, but she said nothing. Meanwhile, her aunt could not understand what was happening around her.

The following night the feast was repeated with yet more spectacular festivities. The whole population was excited. It was the first time in their history that a royal was going to marry a poor woman. The news traveled even beyond the frontiers and was received with yet more amazement.

Days and months passed, and the aunt started complaining that her niece had never invited her or sent her a present. She kept telling people how ungrateful her niece was, since she had been the one who had taken care of her after her mother's death!

A year later the niece gave birth to a son. The aunt seized the opportunity to try to visit her. She told her husband how much she missed her niece; it would be a shame on the family if she did not go to congratulate her niece on the birth of her first child. The father found himself compelled to seek the permission of the sultan's son, and the latter showed no objection.

Thus, the aunt made her preparations for the visit and took her blind daughter along with her. Her niece received her in her private room, and they sat talking intimately. After a while the aunt said, "Oh, my dear niece, come close to me. Let me comb your hair." The niece laid her head on her aunt's lap and relaxed; eventually, she fell asleep. The aunt had seven pins like thin thorns hidden in her sleeve. One by one she skillfully planted them in her niece's head. And with the seventh pin, the niece turned into a white pigeon and flew away in the sky. Immediately, the aunt dressed her own daughter in the niece's clothes and jewelry and settled her in bed. Thus, she concluded her visit.

When the sultan's son arrived, he was surprised that his wife did not meet him at the door as usual. He saw her sitting in bed with the child in her arms. But the child would not stop crying, and she was doing nothing to pacify him. He took his son from her, but still she remained motionless like a box. "Why are you veiled like that and speechless?" he yelled angrily. "Are you in the presence of a stranger?"

When she still did not respond, he became very angry indeed and snatched off the veil. To his horror he saw a different face. He recognized the woman as the blind daughter of the aunt! He finally realized that his so-called mother-in-law had played a dirty trick on him and his wife.

Enraged by the betrayal, he killed the blind girl and chopped her into small pieces. He put the head in the bottom of a sack and filled it with the other pieces and sent it to the aunt with a slave. "The sultan's son has sent you this present," the slave said and left. The aunt was happy. From now on, she thought, she would finally be receiving favors from the sultan's son, whereas she had been completely ignored by her ungrateful niece. In order to show off the favors to her neighbors, she sent each one a piece of the body. When she got to the bottom of the sack, she discovered her daughter's head. She went into shock and was struck dumb.

Every day when the prince went out to do his work, he left his little son playing in the garden. When a flock of birds flew in the sky above him, the child raised his eyes in tears. "O birds!" he asked. "Haven't you seen my dear mother?"

"She will arrive in the next flock, poor child," they replied.

So he waited, his eyes fixed on the blue horizon. When a flock of pigeons arrived, a white one detached herself from them and alighted on the child's head and shoulders. She gently flapped her wings around his head and face. Then she flew up and disappeared in the sky. Thus, every day the child expected the pigeon to visit him and keep him company for a short while. Then she joined the other pigeons.

Not far from the garden an old beggar would sit begging. One day he noticed this scene and overheard the conversation between child and birds. As the prince entered the palace, the old beggar went up to him and told him what he had heard and seen. The prince gave him some alms and went inside.

The next day the prince decided to stay home to see for himself. He took his son to the garden and concealed himself behind some shrubs. He saw and heard exactly what the beggar had told him.

Next morning he painted the head and shoulders of his son with transparent glue, retreated behind the shrubs, and waited. When the white pigeon arrived and landed on the child, she was stuck. The prince sprang out and caught her. He immediately started examining her feathers one by one. Suddenly, his fingers felt thin thorns planted in her skin. He started pulling them out carefully, one by one. As soon as he had taken out the seventh thorn, the pigeon turned into a woman—his very own wife in flesh and blood. She hugged the child and kissed his father.

Thus, they all went in their room, where the prince asked her what had happened. She told him the whole story from beginning to end. He sent his soldiers to arrest the aunt and bring her in for trial. And in a public place she was tied to a tree and burned alive. Afterward, the prince invited the fisherman to live with him and keep an eye on his daughter. Since then they have all lived in peace and happiness.

Rhaida

[5]

RHAIDA WAS A PRINCESS of stunning charm and beauty. She had two brothers: one older and one younger. When she reached the age of ten, her father, the sultan, secluded her from everyone except her mother and younger brother. From that time even her elder brother never set his eyes on her. When her father grew old and died, her brother, the heir, assumed the throne. Rhaida's mother took care of her, and her younger brother was her only companion.

One day the neighboring country waged a war against her brother, the new sultan. He gathered together all the men in his country, exempting only women, children, and old people. Putting on his armor, he rode to the front on his horse.

After he had left, Rhaida pleaded with her mother. "Please, dear mother," she said, "now that there are no men to see me, I'd like to go out and sit just in front of the door so I can see a bit of the world. I've forgotten what the sun, birds, and trees look like."

Her mother agreed.

A few steps away from the door there was a stream of clear water. Rhaida went over to it and sat by the edge. The water was so clean and fresh that she was tempted to wash her hair, which was long enough to cover her back and face completely. While she was combing it, a long hair fell in the stream and was carried away down the stream.

Farther down the same stream her brother the sultan had stopped to let his horse drink. Suddenly, the horse gave a loud snort, raised its head, and started shaking it to left and right. Something seemed to have gotten stuck in his mouth. The sultan's first thought was that it could be a leech. When he opened the horse's mouth to check, he spotted a hair coiling around its tongue and teeth. He pulled it out carefully and stood staring at it with astonishment and admiration, for it was the longest and most beautiful hair he had ever seen in his life. He kept it in his handkerchief and sent for an old woman.

When the old woman arrived, she found the sultan surrounded by his advisers and assistants. Once she had bowed to him, he motioned to her to come closer and showed her the hair. "Find me the owner of this hair," he said, "and I swear by God I will marry her even though she be my own sister, Rhaida!"

His entourage was shocked and alarmed by such a declaration. They all said nothing, but in their hearts they prayed that the hair belonged to someone else. The rumor spread fast, and soon the whole population, except his own family, had heard about the sultan's words. "God forbid!" they all exclaimed and were saddened by the news. A mysterious fear gripped their hearts, and they had an uneasy feeling that the end of the world was near at hand.

The old woman went up the stream, searching all the houses nearby. It did not take long for her to discover who was the owner of the hair. She returned to the sultan with the news, believing that he would change his mind and continue his advance toward the front. But, much to her surprise, to the shock of his advisers, and to the utter indignation of the whole population, he insisted on sticking to his declaration. Adamant in his determination, he turned a deaf ear to all warnings and commanded that preparations be made for the wedding.

When his mother and sister were finally informed of the sultan's intention, they could not believe their ears. But the sultan's word was absolute. So the preparations went ahead throughout the country in spite of everyone's objections.

On the wedding night, Rhaida was sitting in her room with her younger brother, her only companion. "Do you really love me?" she asked him.

"Oh, yes, I do," he replied in a childish voice.

"All right," she said, "then listen to me carefully. When they take me to the sultan's room, you're to come in, steal the comb, and then run away as fast as you can. When I shout 'Stop!' you should keep running. And when I shout 'Run!' stop for me. Understand?"

"Yes."

When the moment came and the slaves were preparing the bride, her younger brother stole into the room, snatched the comb, and escaped. Rhaida ran after him shouting, "Stop! Stop!" They ran farther and farther from the palace until they reached the foot of a mountain. Then she shouted "Run!" and he stopped for her. They both climbed to the top of the mountain and hid themselves among a herd of deer. The trees were so tall and the grass so thick that even the deer were invisible. At night when it grew cold, Rhaida laid her younger brother down on half of her hair and covered him with the other half so as to keep him warm and comfortable.

Meanwhile, back in the palace, slaves and soldiers were all diverted from their tasks to search for the bride. When they found nothing around the palace, the sultan mounted his horse and ordered his soldiers to follow him through the night toward the mountain. At the edge of the thick, impenetrable forest, the sultan started shouting at the top of his voice: "O Rhaida! Come out wherever you are!"

The echo reverberated across the mountain. Many horrible voices were heard, but then another voice echoed back: "Woe to you! I am your sister. Go away! Go away, away. . . !"

For several days he came back alone to the edge of the forest and yelled the name of Rhaida, begging her to come down, but eventually he gave up hope. At that point a messenger arrived with the news that the enemy was drawing close to his palace. Finally, he abandoned the forest in order to defend his territory. But his soldiers were demoralized by the Rhaida incident; most of them had already capitulated. A large part of the country was under the control of the invaders.

That year an unprecedented drought hit the country. People viewed it as a curse; God was angry because the sultan had blasphemed by planning to marry his own sister. As day followed day, the forest where Rhaida and her little brother were living among the deer was losing its trees and grass. The animals were forsaking their refuge for other regions. Streams and springs were drying up; only one spring continued to flow, and that was where the deer drank. When Rhaida's brother was thirsty, she advised him to chew a few of the leaves and blades of grass that were left, warning him not to go near the water in the spring. When he could no longer resist, he went to the spring and drank. Almost immediately, he was turned into a young fawn. When Rhaida discovered the change, it was already too late. Even so, she continued to take care of her brother; every night she wrapped him in her long, thick hair.

Meanwhile, the sultan, who by now had lost a large portion of both his territory and his popularity, shut himself up in his palace. There he pined away in despair and grief. Then came the day when he was found dead in his room.

The forest now looked bald and deserted. When the only remaining spring dried up completely, the flock of deer left their refuge. They traveled farther and farther in search of food and water. Rhaida and her deer brother followed them wherever they went.

Miles away, beyond the frontiers of the realm, the deer found a forest with abundant water and grass. There Rhaida settled, still living in their midst.

In this particular forest human beings were rarely seen because it was full of wild, dangerous beasts. The only person with the courage to frequent it was an old woman who collected medicinal herbs. One day she was resting beside a small lake in the middle of the forest and sorting out the herbs she had gathered. It was around midday when the herd of deer came down to drink. The old woman sat watching them when suddenly she spotted in their midst a strange creature that looked just like a woman with long, dark hair. The old woman set off to see the sultan of that country in order to tell him about the strange phenomenon she had witnessed. When she was admitted to his office, she bowed. "Long live the sultan!" she proclaimed. "May I speak?"

"Proceed," he said, raising his staff. "What has brought you here?"

"My lord," she continued, "in the forest nearby I saw a dazzling light surrounded by a black cloud."

"Speak clearly, woman! I have no time. What is it?"

"A strange creature. She has a face shining like the moon and long, black hair that flows down to her heels, and she lives among the deer."

With that the sultan instructed his guards to search for the creature and catch her as soon as possible. The old woman guided them to the small lake. They concealed themselves in the bush around the lake and waited until the deer came down to drink. Suddenly, in the middle of the flock they saw something that looked like a woman, with a small fawn walking alongside her. The guards pounced on her from all sides, and the deer were frightened away; they fled back into the forest like lightning. The woman was caught and taken to the palace. The small deer doggedly followed behind them. The guards tried to chase it away, but it kept dodging them; eventually, they laughed and ignored it. When they reached the palace, they shut the fawn up in a small hut right by the entrance.

When the sultan saw the strange woman, he asked his slaves to give her a good wash and dress her in decent clothes. He then went out to the court to finish his business. When he returned, he found her seated in the room and radiating beauty and charm. Immediately, he fell in love with her and decided that she should stay in his room and be treated with kindness.

Every night, when she was alone, she looked out the window and spoke to the small deer. "How are you, dear brother?" she would ask.

"O sister!" he used to reply. "It's cold here and I'm not well fed."

She could only weep and beg him to be patient.

One night an aged servant happened to overhear their conversation and reported it to the sultan. The latter checked for himself and then decided to slaughter the deer and roast it.

That night Rhaida opened the window as usual. "O dear brother!" she asked. "How are you?"

"Oh, my sister!" he replied. "The knife is being sharpened, and the fire made ready. People's mouths are watering! I don't have long to live."

The sister wept bitterly. "Do not be afraid," she said. "Anything that happens to you will happen to me, too."

When the old servant reported this conversation to the sultan, he abandoned his plan. He was very curious to know the truth first, and so he summoned Rhaida. "Tell me," he asked, "what's the mystery of that deer?"

So she told him the story from beginning to end. As he listened, tears fell from his eyes. Eventually, he told her, "I shall marry you, and we'll both take care of the fawn."

That made her happy, and her beauty increased in the eyes of the sultan.

The following day the wedding took place. The sultan and Rhaida immediately took the small deer and traveled to the forest where her brother had drunk from the sacred spring. They led the fawn to the spring. Once he had drunk his fill, he became a human being again, a handsome youth. Thus, the three of them returned to the palace where they lived happily ever after.

The Little Sister with Seven Brothers

[6]

ONCE UPON A TIME there was a woman who gave birth only to male children. She felt happy until other women started pestering and laughing at her, saying that she was incapable of producing a daughter. She went on trying until she had seven sons, then she gave up hope. When her sons grew up, other children ridiculed them because they did not have a sister. With time they came to feel miserable. After talking among themselves they decided to broach the topic with their mother. They threatened to leave her if she did not bear a baby girl. She asked them to be patient. In fact, she was already pregnant again and was hoping it would be a girl. It was almost time for the delivery. "All right, Mother," they said. "We'll be waiting on top of the mountain. If it's a girl, hoist a reed spindle; if it's another boy, hoist a stick." Then they went to the mountain and waited anxiously.

When her labors began, she asked her sister to assist her. She told her to hoist a spindle on the roof of the house if it was a girl and a stick if it was a boy. When the baby came, the mother lay down exhausted. Her sister went out and hoisted a stick. The boys saw the signal and went away. After the mother had rested for a while, she turned her head and was delighted to see it was a baby

33

girl. She thanked her God and asked her sister if she had given the boys a signal. She replied that she had. So the mother waited for them to return. She waited all day and all night, but they did not show up. She started suspecting that her sister had given them the wrong signal. Jealousy made her feel betrayed, and she resigned herself to her fate.

Days passed, then months, then years. The daughter was growing up fast. She realized that women were pointing at her and calling her "the little sister with seven brothers." She felt sad and cried to herself. Her father was always busy; he was a traveling salesman who was away from home most of the time.

One day the girl could no longer stand her situation. "Please, Mother," she begged, "tell me why people keep calling me 'the little sister with seven brothers'?"

"Don't pay any attention," her mother answered. "They're just being mean."

But the daughter was not convinced. "Now, listen to me, Mother," she insisted. "If you don't tell me the truth, I'm going to kill myself."

The mother realized she really meant it and was afraid she would lose her last child. So she sat down with her and told her the whole truth.

The daughter kept reflecting on her situation for days, then she reached a decision. "I'm going away to look for my brothers," she told her mother. "Give me a she-camel and two slaves, a male and a female, to accompany me on this journey."

Her mother consulted the father, and they both agreed.

"My daughter," said the father, "go wherever you wish. May you be successful in your mission!"

The mother looked sad, but she had no other choice. She prepared the girl's luggage and enough clothes and food. Then she fixed a *mejoun,* a tiny device like a phone, in her headdress. After wishing her daughter good luck, the party set off on the journey.

The daughter mounted the she-camel, followed by the two slaves and a greyhound. They traveled days and nights until they were far from home. The two slaves were very tired and whispered to each other. They then stood in front of the she-camel. "All right, now," they told the daughter. "We've had enough of being slaves. Get off the camel! It's our turn to ride!"

Just then the girl's father's voice came straight at them with an angry command. "You menials! How dare you? Leave your mistress on the camel, and do as she tells you. Or else I'll kill you!"

They both bowed and continued walking behind her.

Farther on they reached two springs, one white and one black. There they stopped to rest and drink. When the female slave was helping the daughter down, she noticed a tiny box tied near her ear. She guessed it was a *mejoun*, so she snatched it away and shouted to the male slave, "Here's the magic device!"

He immediately smashed it with a rock. From that point all communication between daughter and parents was severed.

Now the slaves made her drink and wash in the black spring, so she turned black on the spot, while they drank and washed in the white spring and became white. From then on, they were free people and she was their slave. Thus, they rode on the she-camel, and she followed behind them with the greyhound. The journey in quest of the brothers continued for many days and nights. Finally, they arrived at a kingdom where her eldest brother was sultan and the other brothers governors in different provinces.

Soon the news reached the sultan that someone was claiming to be his sister. He arrived in person to welcome her. When he saw the she-camel and the greyhound, he recognized both of them and felt reassured. The woman on the camel introduced herself as his sister and the man with her as her husband. The slave simply watched from the side. The sultan embraced his sister and her husband and took them into his palace. He gave them a nice place to live, and their slave was given a small room set apart. Then the sultan sent messages to his brothers, and they all arrived to welcome the sister. Thus, the couple stayed in the palace, enjoying a luxurious life.

One day the sultan's shepherd ran away without notice, leaving the herd of camels unattended. The sultan thought that his sister's slave could take care of the camels. So, he asked his sister and her husband, and they agreed. Hearing the news, the slave was very happy to be free at least from that tiny room.

While she was away in the fields with the camels, she started singing to them the same song every day:

> O camels of my brother!
> How can you eat and drink
> When the free has become slave
> And the slave free?

The camels listened to her intently and started to cry. They stopped eating and drinking. As day followed day, the camels began to look more and more miserable. They were losing weight, and their fur kept falling off in tufts. The sultan noticed this and complained to his sister that her slave was neglecting his camels.

"O brother," she replied, "follow her. If you find her idle, kill her."

So the next day the sultan rode on his horse into the fields. As he approached, he heard the slave singing and saw the camels standing by her. He surprised her and grabbed her by the arm. "Tell me," he demanded, "what's the meaning of those words of yours? Tell me, or I'll kill you!"

She cried bitterly and told him the entire story. And now, for the first time in a whole week, the camels started eating.

The sultan took her back with him. He ordered his soldiers to take the couple and the slave to the two springs. There the couple were forced to drink and wash in the black spring and the slave in the white one. Almost immediately, the couple became black and the slave white. Then the soldiers took them back to the palace.

Finally, the sultan and his brothers welcomed their real sister and sentenced the two slaves to be burned and buried in a *metmoura*, or hole. The sister was given a luxurious room to live in, and slaves had to serve her. Thereafter, her brothers visited her almost every day and brought her presents.

Meanwhile, the brothers' wives were getting jealous and started conspiring to get rid of her. One day they met in the garden and invited her to join them. One of the wives brought food and a single egg. She showed it to the other wives. "You see this egg?" she said. "The woman who can swallow it is the one who loves her brothers the most."

They all struggled, trying to snatch it from her. But the sultan's sister challenged them. "Give it to me," she said. "No one loves her brothers more than I do!"

They let her have it. "You're the winner!" they all said.

Days went by, and the sultan started noticing some changes in his sister's figure. The women kept dropping hints and gesturing in her direction. As the rumor spread, the sultan's suspicion kept growing day by day. Then one day, as he sat chatting with his sister, he asked her to comb his hair. Resting his head on her lap, he listened carefully and could feel something strange moving inside her womb. His worst suspicions were thus confirmed, and he felt ashamed and humiliated.

Next day he threw her out with harsh words and no explanation: "Go back home, you—!"

He summoned a slave and ordered him to accompany her. In fact, he had already instructed him to take her to a wild and deserted place and leave her there.

The slave accomplished his mission and returned to the palace. The sister was left crying on her own, at the mercy of rain and wind. For days and nights she suffered with no food or shelter. One day a horseman came riding by and found her in desperate straits. He stopped and asked her what had brought her there. When she told him her story, he took pity on her and brought her to his house. His wife was frightened when she first saw the girl, but he explained everything and she welcomed her guest.

The wife took care of her. While she was washing her one day, she felt something coiling inside her womb. She told her husband, and they discussed the case. As an experienced couple they were able to guess what her problem was. The following morning the husband brought a sheep and slew it. His wife oversalted the meat and then roasted it. Then they invited their guest to eat as much as she could. After a while she started complaining that there was too much salt on the meat, but they urged her to eat more and more until she was burning with thirst. They refused to give her any water and insisted that she should eat more. When she could no longer go on, the wife brought a large bowl of cold water and placed it in front of her, but would not let her touch it. The husband brought a rope, tied her feet, and hoisted her, head downward, up to a tree branch high above the ground. Then the wife placed the bowl underneath her mouth. Her thirst reached its climax, and she started writhing and crying like a baby. Even so, the couple just watched and waited. Suddenly, snakes started leaping out of her mouth and dropping into the bowl of water. When they had counted seven of them, they released her and gave her water to drink. And now she finally realized that the egg she had swallowed was a snake's egg.

After resting for a while, she expressed her gratitude to the couple and told them where her brother the sultan and her other brothers were. The man wrote the sultan a letter and sent it by carrier pigeon.

Soon her brother the sultan received the message. He gathered together all his brothers in a secret meeting and read the letter to them. They were shocked. Leaping on their horses, they rushed off to bring back their sister.

Once they had returned, their wives were astonished to see their sister looking so cheerful and in normal condition. The seven wives were all brought before the court, condemned, and executed in public. The sister and her brothers lived happily ever after.

The Treasure

[7]

LONG, LONG AGO there lived two brothers, one rich and the other very poor. Instead of helping his brother, the rich one poked fun at him in public and humiliated him. One day the poor brother was in utter despair, since he was unable to feed his wife and numerous children. He decided to put an end to his misery.

He put on his *boundaf*, a short, tattered gown, and climbed to the summit of a high mountain. There he stood with his eyes wide open to the sky. Raising his hands in prayer, he addressed God: "O God! Why have you made me so miserable? Why this injustice? If you don't get me out of this dire situation, I shall kill myself."

Removing his gown he started furiously lashing out at the rock until he collapsed, unconscious. He had no idea how long he slept. When he opened his eyes, he saw beside him a hen laying golden eggs. He could not believe his eyes. When he touched the eggs to make sure, he was very happy and grateful to God. He took the hen and the eggs and went home. "Cheer up!" he told his wife. "God is merciful. He has made us rich forever." He told her to keep the hen a secret from everyone.

Thereafter, the hen laid a golden egg every day. On market days he collected the eggs and sold them in order to buy everything they needed. After a few trips to the market he became very rich and started buying cattle and land. Neighbors noticed the change in his lifestyle and started wondering what fortune he had come upon. But the source of wealth remained a mystery to them, and he enjoyed the secret.

One day he was in a hurry to go to market to do some business and could not wait for the hen to lay eggs. So he decided to take the hen to market with him. His wife disapproved of the idea, but he reassured her: "Don't worry, no one will find out."

Once he got to the market, he thought of taking a walk around first to see what he could buy. On the edge of the market he had a friend, a hairdresser who worked in a tent. He was the only friend he could trust with the hen without arousing suspicion. "Can I leave this hen with you for a while?" he asked his friend in as casual a manner as possible. Without bothering to look, the hairdresser pointed to a corner. "I hope it won't make too much of a mess," he commented jokingly. Like many other people, the hairdresser had noticed how rich his friend had become but had never asked any questions. Once he was left alone with the hen, he kept staring at it. There was nothing unusual about it. Suddenly, the hen started cackling. He guessed it had laid an egg and went to see. He was surprised to discover that the egg was shining like gold. He held it in his hand and realized that it was indeed real gold. He looked around and thought fast.

The hairdresser quickly went out, bought an identical hen, and left it in his tent. The real one he took home with him and hid. When his friend returned from his rounds in the market, he thanked the hairdresser and returned home with the wrong hen. He and his wife waited for the hen to lay an egg, but, when it did, it was only an ordinary one. It was then he realized he had been cheated by the hairdresser, but he kept quiet about the entire matter. His wife was very angry, but he pacified her. "Don't worry," he said. "God is just and merciful."

The following day he went back to the same mountain and did what he had done before. When he opened his eyes again, he did not see a hen but only two clubs standing erect right in front of him. They started beating him until he cried out in pain. He accepted them as a gift from God. "I submit," he said. "I'll take you."

He returned home, carrying the two clubs under his gown. When his wife saw them, she was frightened. But he kept them in his room and did not leave home for many days. Then one day he went back to the market, concealing the two clubs. He passed by his friend's tent and greeted him as usual. The hairdresser saw that he was hiding something under his gown and asked what it was. The poor man said it was a secret and asked if he might leave it in his tent for a while. The hairdresser agreed and hid the two clubs in a corner. The poor man pretended to leave but actually hid behind the tent and waited to see what would happen.

After a short while the two clubs raised themselves and started beating the hairdresser. He kept crying and begging them to stop. When the poor man felt his friend had been beaten enough, he entered the tent again. "Where is my hen?" he yelled. "If you don't bring it back to me, those clubs will kill you."

The hairdresser admitted his deceit and ran to his house, with the two clubs in hot pursuit. They kept beating him until he returned the hen to its owner.

Father and Daughters

[8]

ONCE UPON A TIME there lived a man who had seven daughters and only one son. When his wife died, he was left bereft and grief-stricken, and bearing a heavy responsibility. Seeing him in such a miserable state, his friends advised him to go on the pilgrimage in order to forget his worries. He decided to take his son with him as a companion. However, the thought of leaving his daughters on their own worried him so much that he looked perpetually sad and pensive.

His daughters noticed his mood. "What troubles you, Father?" they asked.

"Well," he replied, "I'm going on the pilgrimage. My real problem is that I have seven eggs, and I don't know what to do with them. If I take them with me, they might break, but if I leave them here, I'm afraid they'll go rotten."

"I'll boil them for you," one of them suggested. "Then they won't spoil."

"I'll fry them," suggested another.

The other daughters had still different ideas, but none of them satisfied him. Finally, the youngest daughter, named Fatna, arrived. "What is bothering you, Father?" she asked.

He repeated what he had told the other sisters and waited for her idea. But she did not reply at first and thought for a while. Eventually, she declared, "I understand what you mean, Father. The seven eggs are ourselves. Don't trouble yourself. Build us an iron door and provide us with all the food we need for the period of your journey. Then everything will be fine."

At last he brightened up. "That's what I wanted to hear," he told her.

The next day he did exactly as his youngest daughter had suggested. When all the arrangements for the journey had been made, he remembered a bed of basil just outside the door. He wondered who would water it during his absence in order to keep it alive. Since the youngest daughter was the one who understood him, he chose her to take care of the basil. He then spoke to the other daughters: "Now, I am going to leave. Only Fatna is allowed to go outside once in a while to water the basil. You have everything you need, so there is no reason to go out. Good-bye."

Once he had left with his son, the youngest daughter started going out to tend to the bed of basil. One day the sultan's son and heir was on an errand and saw the girl watering the bed of basil. She attracted his attention, and he stopped his horse to talk to her. "O Fatna, daughter of al-Hajj!" he said. "How many leaves are in that bed of basil?"

"As many as the words in your books."

Of course, she had heard that he was well read and a real bookworm. He was amazed by her intelligent response. He repeated his question.

She changed her response. "As many leaves as stars in the sky," she said.

Reflecting for a moment, he understood her hint. For him it meant she was as unattainable as a star. He felt snubbed and went away unhappy. He looked for an old woman and consulted her about the matter: "Please, tell me: how can I win the heart of

Fatna, daughter of the Hajj? I talked to her, but she gave me the cold shoulder. What can I do?"

The old woman reflected on the matter and proposed her scheme. He was satisfied.

A fly immediately flew to Fatna. It told her what the sultan's son had done and explained the whole scheme the old woman had devised. Fatna understood it all and nodded her head with a smile.

A few days later, an old woman was seen heading toward the sisters' house; she was accompanied by a well-dressed girl whose face was covered by a black veil. The fly landed on Fatna's ear and hummed something to her. Fatna gathered her sisters together. "Listen!" she told them urgently. "I'm not feeling well. I have a fever. I'm going to lie down. If anyone knocks at the door, don't open it. Beware, beware!"

And with that she went to her bed and pretended to fall asleep.

A few minutes later a knock was heard at the door.

"Who is it?" the sisters asked.

"Your aunt and her daughter," the old woman answered. "Open the door. We've come for a visit."

The voice of a woman convinced the sisters that there was no danger, so they opened the door. The old woman and her daughter came in. The woman started asking them how they were coping in the absence of their father and whether they needed any help. Fatna was watching and listening carefully, pretending to be asleep. When the old woman realized that Fatna was lying asleep, she asked the other sisters, "Oh, Fatna is sick, isn't she?"

They replied that she had a fever. The aunt showed great sympathy and was ready to help her because she always carried some medicine with her. "Come on, girls," she said. "Prepare a meal and a hot drink. I have the cure for Fatna."

The sisters went into the kitchen and prepared some food and tea. The old woman's daughter stayed very quiet all the time, watching Fatna out of the corner of her eye. The old woman apologized to the sisters because her daughter was very shy.

When the meal was ready, the old woman spoke to the other girls. "Now, come and eat," she said in a motherly tone. "Let Fatna rest for a while. I'll take care of her later."

The sisters ate and suddenly fell asleep. When Fatna saw her sisters lying side by side and dead still, she jumped out of bed. "Is this why you've come?" she yelled at her two guests. "I know you both and I know your purpose. Now, get out of here!"

She pushed them out of the door with all her power, so much so that the sultan's son tripped over the doorstep and broke his hip. Fatna closed the door and returned to her sisters. She quickly boiled some herbs in a kettle and made them a drink. Little by little they started to regain consciousness. She scolded them for not heeding her warning.

The following day she put on her father's gown and veil and mounted the mule. She rode until she got to the dwelling of the sultan's son. There she found him sitting in the garden with his private secretary to whom he was dictating a letter.

"Tell her father," Fatna heard him say, "that his daughter Fatna has become a bad woman. No respectable man will ever accept her."

"Peace be upon you," Fatna said, and they returned the greeting. The sultan's son raised his eyes to see a young man sitting upright on the back of a mule like a traveler.

She introduced herself as a *fakih*. "What's wrong with this young man?" she asked the secretary.

He told her his hip was fractured.

"All right," responded the *fakih* with great self-assurance. "Forget about that letter and let me take care of his hip. I have the cure for him."

But the sultan's son insisted on finishing the message first, because it was an urgent matter. He immediately instructed his secretary to dispatch it to Mecca with a special messenger.

Afterward, the *fakih* was invited in. He started examining the hip. He applied a few herbs and made a bandage. The son was made to lie down in bed and stay still for a long time.

When the sultan arrived and found his son feeling better, he invited the *fakih* to stay until his son was completely healed. The *fakih* could not refuse the invitation and was offered a room and food. The next morning the son felt much better; he could stand and walk without any help. He went to see his mother. She was delighted that her son's condition had improved so quickly. "You and the *fakih*," she said, "eat and drink whatever you wish."

In fact, the son had sought out his mother to tell her a secret. He motioned to her. "Mother," he whispered, "I came to tell you that the *fakih* has a scholar's head, but the eyes of Fatna, the Hajj's daughter."

His mother only laughed. "You are just crazy about that girl," she said. "This one's a real *fakih*. The proof is that he has cured you and is knowledgeable about religion and science. Go my son, go!"

But her son was cocksure and ignored what his mother said. He insisted.

"Very well, son," she said eventually. "It's easy to find out if the *fakih* is a man or a woman. Both of you go to the market and buy a sheep's stomach. I'll make it into a dinner dish for you. Women love sheep's stomach. If he eats a lot, she is a woman; if not, he's a man."

The fly buzzed around the *fakih*'s head and disappeared again. The *fakih* gave a smile.

The son asked the *fakih* to accompany him to the market. They bought the stomach and returned home. In the evening the mother offered them the meal. They started eating, and the son kept his eye on the *fakih*. But the latter picked up only a small piece and said thank you. The son insisted.

"Frankly," the *fakih* replied, "I don't like sheep's stomach. It doesn't agree with me. Only women like it."

The son had to return the plate almost untouched to his mother.

"So," she said, "it was just your imagination. Didn't I tell you so?"

But the son was still not convinced. "Mother," he insisted, "that *fakih* has the head of a scholar but the eyes of Fatna, the daughter of the Hajj."

Next day the mother thought of another way of ending her son's suspicion. She proposed, "Today, invite the *fakih* for a swim in the river. This time you'll see with your own eyes. Go my son, go!"

The fly flew around the *fakih's* ears and disappeared again. The *fakih* nodded his head.

When it was hot, the son casually said to the *fakih*, "What do you think of going for a swim in the river?"

The *fakih* readily welcomed the invitation. He rode on his mule and followed the sultan's son on his horse. On their way there, the *fakih* whispered to the fly that landed on the mule's ears and hummed, "When we get to the river, he will start taking off his clothes first. And when our mistress starts, run away. When I shout 'Stop' you should run, and when I shout 'Run' you should stop."

Once in the river, the sultan's son took off his clothes and the *fakih* followed suit. But as soon as he began, the mule started off, running like mad. The *fakih* was shouting aloud, "Stop, Stop!" and he ran fast after it. The sultan's son had to put on his clothes first, then he jumped on his horse and followed them. But the *fakih* had already disappeared on his mule.

When Fatna reached her home, she immediately went in and locked the door behind her. The sultan's son looked everywhere, then he turned to the Hajj's house and stopped by the door to listen, but everything was quiet. Having lost any track of the *fakih*, he returned to the palace dejected.

A few days later, Fatna's brother arrived from Mecca looking very sad. He told his youngest sister of the letter his father had received and the task he had assigned him to accomplish. "Go back home, my son," the father had said. "Take your sister to the valley and slay her. Open her stomach with your knife and bring me her liver and clothes as a token."

He told his sister the whole truth because she was very dear to him.

"O brother," she told her brother as soon as she had heard what he said, "I'm ready. Do as Father told you. But remember that I'm innocent. I've done nothing wrong."

So, her brother took her on his horse and went down to the valley. A greyhound followed them. In the valley he slew the greyhound, removed its liver, and wrapped it in a piece of cloth. Then he asked his sister to bury herself in the sand and take off all her clothes. He hid behind a rock and waited until she said she was ready. Her clothes were in a pile near her, and only her head remained uncovered. He took her clothes and the liver and rode away on his horse back to Mecca.

The sister was left buried in the sand completely naked. There she lay in the burning sun, not knowing what to do next. She could not walk back home naked; she had no hope of going back home in any case, since she was supposed to be dead. So, yielding to her fate, she shut her eyes and fell half-asleep for a while.

Suddenly, a hoof crunched the sand right beside her head and threw it in her face. When she screamed, a horse shied away and almost threw its rider. The man stopped. Turning around he saw the face of a woman. "Curse be upon the devil," he said. "If you're the daughter of this world, show me your fingers. If you're a she-devil, let me go free."

"In the name of God and his Prophet," she replied, "I'm a human being. Fear nothing."

The horseman dismounted and approached her. Bending down, he looked closely at her face.

"Come out of the sand," he said.

"I can't," she replied in embarrassment. "I don't have any clothes."

He then took off his bernous and threw it over her. Turning his face away, he waited for her to extricate herself from the sand.

"All right," she said. "I'm ready now." She sat down, wrapped in the bernous.

"Wait here for a while until I come back," he told her. "I won't be long."

Jumping on his horse he raced to the house and came back with some women's clothes and shoes. Once she had dressed herself, he took her back to the house on his horse. He asked his servant to boil water and wash her. But she refused to let the servant see her. When she came out of the bath, she looked astonishingly beautiful, and he immediately fell in love with her.

"Will you marry me?" he asked.

"I wasn't born to marry," she replied. "I was born to teach the Holy Book and pray with people. I'm a *fakih.*"

She took the man aside and talked to him. He nodded his head. "I understand," he said. He gave her some of his clothes, so she was disguised as a man. She thanked him and went out to the tribe, introducing herself as a *fakih* who was looking for a job in a mosque. People welcomed the new, young *fakih*.

When the time for afternoon prayer came, the *fakih* performed the call to prayer. Afterward, he gathered the children and started teaching them the Qur'an in a large room attached to the mosque. In the evening, after prayer, people gathered around the new *fakih* and listened to religious instruction. They were very pleased and impressed by his knowledge and offered him residence and food.

Days went by and the people kept discussing and praising the sterling qualities of the newcomer. There was one thing, though, that bothered them: a *fakih* was supposed to be married. The following day one of the tribal dignitaries arrived to visit the *fakih* in his residence, accompanied by his most beautiful daughter. They all sat down.

"This is my daughter," the man said. "I offer her to you in marriage."

The daughter sat there, very shy and quiet. The *fakih* reflected for a moment. "It's an honor for me," he responded without hesitation, "and I offer you my thanks. I will take her as my wife according to the Sunna of Allah and his Prophet. Tomorrow we'll arrange the marriage."

Next day the man returned with his daughter and a few witnesses. The ceremony took place in the house of the *fakih*, and the contract was written and signed. The residents soon heard about the happy event and showered the new couple with gifts. The *fakih* expressed his deep gratitude and showed great happiness.

That night the *fakih* sat down to talk to his bride so that they could become more familiar with each other. "You are very welcome, my dear," he said, welcoming the shy girl in a sweet tone. "Eat and drink at ease. This is your home now. But first you must swear on this Holy Book never to betray our private life to anyone."

The bride agreed, placed her hand on the Qur'an, and swore. Then the *fakih* took off his veil for the first time, and the girl saw the beautiful face of a woman.

"As you can see," the *fakih* said, "I'm a woman like you. There is nothing to fear." Then she told the girl the whole story and the reasons for her disguise. She reminded her of the oath they had taken. From then on they lived together happily and peacefully.

Once the pilgrimage ceremonies were over, Fatna's father and brother returned home after a long absence. One day Fatna's father had an argument with the sultan's son over some merchandise, and they both lost their tempers. The father raised his voice, accusing the sultan's son of having been responsible for the tragic loss of his beloved daughter.

When the sultan heard of the quarrel, he investigated the matter and found out the real cause. However, the case was a difficult one to settle. They had to look for a qualified *fakih* to judge them.

The sultan's advisers had heard of a *fakih* somewhere in another tribe who had acquired a high reputation; travelers everywhere talked about him as a man of knowledge, intelligence, and imagination. And so it was there that the sultan took his son and Fatna's father.

When they all arrived at that tribe, it was already nighttime. The *fakih* welcomed them with hospitality and offered them food and his house to spend the night. He told them he would consider their problem the next morning after the first prayer. With that the *fakih* went to his wife and told her about his guests. He slaughtered a chicken and prepared a good meal.

The *fakih* and his guests sat down in the front of the mosque and talked. He asked them where they had come from and what was their problem. When the evening prayer came, he climbed the minaret of the mosque and announced the call to prayer. The inhabitants gathered, and they all prayed together. Then the *fakih* took his guests to his house for dinner.

During the meal the sultan's son started having suspicions about the *fakih*. After dinner they all slept in one large room. The candle was extinguished.

"Tell me stories," the *fakih* asked. That was the custom of people in those days, since they had no other means of entertainment. And they all had tales to tell.

The guests insisted that the *fakih* should start. So he told them the story of a daughter who was falsely accused of bad conduct. In the story the daughter told the sultan's son, "I wouldn't marry you even if you knew all the secrets of the stars."

With every new detail the son's suspicion was growing. When the father who accused him of slandering his daughter heard the tale, he started feeling responsible for her death.

"Please, stop!" he exclaimed suddenly. "That's enough." And he started weeping.

When the *fakih* realized that his story had its intended effect, he lit the candle again. "Does your daughter bear any mark?" the *fakih* asked. "Would you be able to recognize her if you saw her again?"

"Alas!" he replied. "She's dead now. But I remember when she was a child, she fell on a rock and cut her forehead. The scar is like a crescent."

Whereupon the *fakih* took off his turban and veil. The man saw both the mark and the full face of his own daughter. He could not contain his joy. He leaped up to embrace her and started kissing her as his tears bathed her face. The sultan's son remained frozen to the spot, while his father was struck dumb with astonishment. She explained to them that her story was true.

Next morning, after dawn prayer, they all left home. The sultan's son confessed the whole truth. When they were back home, the sultan put his son on trial and sentenced him to death, but Fatna pardoned him. The sultan accepted her plea and let his son go free. Then the Hajj put his daughter on his horse and went home feeling very happy.

The Jealous Mother

[9]

ONCE UPON A TIME there was an extraordinarily beautiful woman, her beauty equal only to that of the moon itself. When she was married and got pregnant, she used to go out at night and address the moon. "O moon," she would say, "you and I are both beautiful, so beautiful that no one can compete with us."

The moon would answer her. "True, you and I are beautiful," it would reply, "but the one still in your womb is yet more beautiful. She will outshine us."

The mother started to worry about her future as the most beautiful woman on earth. When the time approached for her to give birth, she called in a midwife she trusted. She asked her to bury the baby as soon as it was delivered and to replace it with a puppy dog. She gave her a lot of gold, and so the matter was settled.

The midwife produced a puppy and laid it beside the mother. She then took the baby girl away, but, instead of burying her, she kept her secluded inside her house and took care of her.

The woman's husband came home. "Just look at what God has given us," she said. "A puppy dog!"

The man was stunned. Fearing the public shame, he immediately threw the dog away.

The midwife raised the baby girl in secret until she grew to the age of ten. It was only then that some people in the neighborhood set eyes on her and started talking about an astonishingly beautiful girl. The midwife claimed that it was her own daughter. She named her Lalla Khallalt El Khoudra. Whenever people mentioned a beautiful woman, they would say, "She is not as beautiful as Lalla." Thus, her name was on everyone's tongue. In time the rumor reached the ears of her real mother, and she began to suspect the midwife.

One day she approached her. "Can you please send me your daughter?" she asked. "She can help me disentangle a ball of wool thread."

The old woman agreed and, in exchange for a handful of gold, sent her daughter.

When the real mother set eyes on the girl, her heart started writhing with jealousy. She gave the girl a large ball of thread and asked her to stretch it until it was completely untied. Lalla walked farther and farther, day and night, until she found herself in a strange environment—the land of ghouls. When her mother guessed she had walked that far, she cut the thread. Now Lalla could not find her way back home.

Night had already fallen. Lalla started looking around for a shelter to spend the night. She soon realized she was in the midst of strange creatures that looked like the ghouls in tales she had heard from the old midwife. Scared of being eaten alive, she climbed onto a roof and hid herself among the thatch. It was not long before she discovered that her hiding place was the house of seven ghoul brothers, all bachelors. All they had was a slave who cooked for them.

Early in the morning the ghouls went out to hunt. The slave remained behind alone to prepare their food. All of a sudden she heard something up on the roof, and, looking up, she saw a very beautiful face staring down at her. "If you're a human being," the slave exclaimed, "say so. But if you are a jinn, go away."

"I am a miserable human being," Lalla replied. "I'm dying of hunger and thirst. Please help me."

The slave now invited her down and gave her some food and water. But she warned her that the owners of the dwelling were seven dangerous ghouls; she advised her to stay out of sight, or else they would eat her up.

So Lalla went back to her hiding place. Every day, when the ghouls went out, the slave invited Lalla to join her and taught her how to cook. Lalla learned fast and was very useful to the slave.

As day followed day, the ghouls began to notice a difference in the cooking; it tasted better and better. A new flavor had been added to their food. They discussed this new change among themselves and decided that the next day the youngest brother should stay behind and conceal himself in a hiding place to see what the slave was adding to the food.

The other six brothers left. The slave woke up and as usual called Lalla down from her hiding place. They started cooking together, but now Lalla was doing most of the work while the slave relaxed. The youngest ghoul waited for a while, but then he jumped out from his hiding place and surprised them both. Lalla was frightened and remained glued to the spot. But the ghoul spoke very softly to her, assuring her that she would not be harmed. To the contrary he gave her a warm and friendly welcome. As soon as his eyes looked at her, he fell in love and decided to marry her.

When his brothers returned, he met them at the door and told them what had happened. They all sat down and discussed the matter. They agreed to give the couple a great wedding ceremony the very next day.

With the presence of such a charming beauty their life had been completely transformed into a paradise. They were all very happy.

Thereafter, all of the seven brothers' care and attention were devoted to Lalla. She was the one who did the cooking, and the slave was now left neglected. Day after day she became more and more jealous. "Promise me," she said to Lalla one day, "that you will share everything with me." Lalla agreed and swore an oath on it.

Everything went according to plan. The slave slept most of the time, and Lalla did the housework. One day, while Lalla was preparing the food, she came upon a broad bean. She ate half and nudged the slave to give her the other half, but the slave pretended to be sound asleep and did not wake up. After a while, she gave a yawn. "Weren't you nudging me a while ago," she asked Lalla, "or was I dreaming?"

"Yes," replied Lalla cheerfully, "I've half of a bean for you."

She felt her headscarf and untied a knot where she had hidden it, but to her disappointment and horror she could not find it. The slave complained that she had broken her promise and reprimanded her.

In the evening the slave took her revenge. She poured water on the fire, so when time came to prepare the food for the ghouls, Lalla had no fire. Afraid that they would be angry, she begged the slave to help her find some fire. Time was running out, and soon the ghouls would be returning home. The slave told her to go out and borrow some fire from a neighbor.

So Lalla went out to the dwelling of an old ghoul named Uncle Yazit, who was notorious for his ferocity and cunning. But Lalla knew nothing about him. She knocked on his door and waited. He looked outside. "What do you want?" he asked. "Why are you crying?"

"Uncle . . ."

"Yazit. Uncle Yazit."

"Uncle Yazit, please give me some fire quickly."

"Oh, is that all you want? You can have as much as you want. But first, do you want me to pierce your stomach with a red-hot nail, or do you prefer to be marked on the forehead with a sharp knife?"

She stood there stunned, not knowing what to do. He yawned, and she could see his teeth arrayed like sharp knives.

"Make your mind up," he said in a tone of menace, "or I'll—."

She chose to be marked. He handed her the fire and then cut her forehead until blood started streaming down. She turned away and headed back home apace, with the blood dropping behind her and marking her path. Suddenly, a pigeon appeared and tried to dry her blood with her wings, but Lalla thought it was playing with her and shooed it away. "Oh, please, leave me alone now!" she cried. "I'm so miserable and don't feel like playing."

The next day Uncle Yazit followed the drops of blood until he found her door. He knocked. "Give me your finger," he said, "or I'll eat you."

She pushed her finger through the keyhole. He sucked some of her blood, then left.

And so, every day Uncle Yazit visited Lalla and sucked some of her blood. Gradually, she started feeling weak and looking pale. Her deteriorating health affected her work and cooking. The ghoul brothers started to notice the change in both her behavior and the taste of her food. They wondered why she was looking so miserable and pensive all the time. Wasn't she happy? Did she miss her home? Weren't they kind enough to her? They always did their best to make her feel comfortable and to bring her everything she wished. So what was going wrong with her? They discussed the matter among themselves and agreed to leave the youngest behind to watch her. He concealed himself somewhere and kept an eye on her movements. In the evening he heard a knock at the door. Lalla went to answer it. Uncle Yazit had come on his usual visit, and she pushed her finger through the keyhole. He sucked her blood and left. Meanwhile, the youngest ghoul just watched from his hiding place and kept quiet. He could not confront Uncle Yazit on his own even if he wanted to.

He waited until his other brothers came back and told them what he had seen. They discussed the problem and made their plan. Next day they decided not to go hunting. Lalla and the slave were both surprised to see them staying home. They asked the ghouls what was wrong, but they simply answered that they were having a rest day. The house was very quiet.

The time came for Uncle Yazit's daily visit. When he asked Lalla for her finger, the youngest brother sprang beside her. "Tell him to go away," he whispered in her ear, "or he'll be destroyed."

"Your finger, or I'll eat you!" Yazit yelled.

Lalla answered as she was instructed. Yazit repeated his demand yet more threateningly, but still she dismissed him with harsh words. When his anger reached its peak, he forced open the door, and it gave way. He fell into a *metmoura*, the trap the brothers had dug during the night and covered with hay. Now they sprang from their corners and looked down at him. "Now, Uncle Yazit," they shouted in unison, "you're going to rise from that hole in smoke!"

Then they called out for Lalla. "How dare you allow a stranger to visit you during our absence?" they yelled at her angrily. "You've betrayed us!"

They threatened to send her after Yazit and meet the same fate. But she started weeping and told them the whole story.

They looked at the slave and saw her trembling. They dragged her by her hair and flung her down into the pit with Yazit. They piled wood over them and lit the fire. The smoke rose until nothing was left but black ashes.

Then they resumed their normal life, going out hunting every day while Lalla busied herself preparing their food.

Little by little she recovered her health and serenity. Her complexion was rosy, and that brightened up the brothers' life like a magic candle. They enjoyed her charm, and all felt happy again. Every day they showered her with gold and silver. They all loved and worshiped her like a goddess who made them human. By now her room was piled high with precious presents.

One day a Jew, a wandering merchant, passed by the house, yelling, "Sweets! Clothes! Cosmetics! Everything you need!" When he heard a voice from inside the house, he stopped his donkey. He led his donkey over to the door and waited. Lalla came out, and he showed her his wares. She chose a few things and asked him for the price. He said he was exchanging his goods for wool, old copper, or silver utensils. She went in and filled a whole sack with silver and gold and gave it to him. He was amazed at her generosity and asked for her name. She said, "Lalla Khallalt El Khoudra," and then asked him, "Do you know a tribe called So-and-so?"

He said he was much traveled, because his trade took him everywhere. So naturally he knew that tribe only too well.

"Please," she begged him, "if you go back to that tribe, ask for a woman called Fulana. She's my mother. Please give her my greetings and tell her I miss her so much."

The Jew promised and departed, still yelling, "Sweets! Clothes! Cosmetics! Everything you need!"

A few months later, his travels brought him to the tribe where her mother lived. An old but beautiful woman called out to him so she could buy a few things, and she paid him with a handful of wool. When he saw what she was offering him, he laughed at her. "Oh," he said, "you're not like Lalla Khallalt El Khoudra who gave me a sack of gold and silver for half of what you have bought."

It was then he remembered the promise he had given Lalla. "Oh," he went on with a sigh, "her beauty surpasses that of the moon itself!"

He was about to ask the old woman if she knew a woman named Fulana, when the goods she bought fell from her hands on the ground. "Please," her mother said, "tell me more about her. I'm her mother."

The Jew was surprised. "She sends you her warmest greetings," he said. "She misses you so much."

"Tell me," the woman insisted, "how is she? Where does she live?"

"She lives in the country of ghouls. But she has become their queen. They worship her and serve her like slaves. They give her all the gold in the world. She is very happy, the richest and the most beautiful woman I've ever seen in my life."

"When will you see her again?"

"Very soon, for sure. Perhaps in a month or two."

The old woman asked him to wait. She went in her house and searched for a present to send her dear daughter. She wrapped a ring in a handkerchief and handed it to the Jew: "Please, give her this. Tell her it's a token from her mother who loves her so much. Tell her to put it under her tongue when she is cooking to protect her against the evil eye."

The Jew promised to convey the message and went on his way.

Two months later the Jew found himself back in the country of ghouls. He remembered the message and went straight to Lalla's house. She was delighted to see him again. She chose a few goods and paid him with another sack of gold and silver. He told her he had seen her mother who was very happy to hear about her. He then produced the present she had sent her and repeated what her mother had advised her to do with it. Lalla wept with joy and kissed the handkerchief in which the ring was stored. She sighed and said she would do as her mother suggested. Then the Jew left to carry on his business.

When Lalla sat down to prepare the meal for the brothers, she untied the handkerchief and put the ring under her tongue. A short while later, she fell into a swoon and remained in a coma looking as still as death. When the ghouls returned home, they found her frozen to the spot. They shook her, but she remained motionless. They cried the whole night and ate nothing.

Next day they made her an *attoush*, a sort of couch all made of gold and silver and her best jewelry, and laid her down in it. They called their camels and asked each of them one by one: "How long can you carry Lalla?"

"One year," one said.

"Ten years," another said.

"As long as I live," said a third with the name Naala (or Shoe).

So the ghouls fixed the *attoush* firmly on the back of the third she-camel. "Do not stop for anyone," they told the camel. "Roam the world. Remember your secret name is Naala. Respond only to this name."

The she-camel agreed and departed.

Naala traveled very far, from one place to another, stopping only to eat and drink and never allowing anyone to come close to her. She crossed deserts, valleys, rivers, and jungles. She saw all sorts of nations until she reached a territory that was ruled by a famous, rich sultan. When his soldiers saw a she-camel carrying something shiny, they informed him and then chased the camel everywhere. But all their efforts were in vain. The sultan consulted all his magicians, who were helpless in the face of this phenomenon.

As the sultan was riding on his horse toward his palace, he heard an old woman laughing. He stopped his horse. "Why are you laughing, old woman?" he asked.

"All your soldiers and magicians can't catch a she-camel as old as I am!"

"Do you mean you can catch her?"

"Old as I am, I will bring her to you."

"Listen, woman! If you do, I'll make you rich forever. If not, I'll kill you. Now go!"

They all ridiculed the old woman and considered her as good as dead anyway. Some said she had nothing to lose. She started running in the direction of the she-camel. Suddenly, she lost one of her shoes and started yelling, "My shoe! Shoe! Shoe!" The she-camel heard her and stopped. She kneeled down and waited for the old woman.

Everyone stood there astonished, including the sultan who now believed she had some supernatural powers. The she-camel was then brought into the palace. When the *attoush* was carefully searched, they discovered inside the corpse of a sleeping beauty. The sultan asked his physicians to examine the body thoroughly. They noticed a strange ring stuck under her tongue. When they removed it, the beautiful woman uttered a scream like a newborn baby and started breathing. Gradually, she regained consciousness and opened her eyes. The sultan was struck by her extraordinary beauty and decided to marry her.

Naala the she-camel was taken inside the palace and taken care of. The slaves took Lalla to the bath and gave her a good bath. The following day the sultan took her for his wife.

Days went by, but Lalla never forgot the seven ghoul brothers. Every day she went out and addressed her camel. "How are your feet?" she would ask. "Did you have a good rest?"

When the she-camel's feet healed and she was ready for another journey, Lalla made her preparations secretly.

One very early morning the sultan had to go to the court for an urgent meeting. Lalla waited for a little while, then slipped away from her room. She took the *attoush*, fixed it on the camel's back, and settled herself in it. "Now don't answer anyone at all," she whispered to the camel.

They fled from the palace. When the soldiers saw her running like a shadow, they informed the sultan. He ordered them to chase her. They did their best, but it was impossible to catch up with her. They gave up and returned to the palace empty-handed. The she-camel went farther and farther without stopping, through deserts, valleys, rivers, and jungles, until she finally reached the territory of the ghouls.

The seven brothers were still in mourning, keeping themselves shut up inside their house. Then all of a sudden, as the camel approached, Lalla let out a loud cry. When they heard her, they all sprang to their feet and went out to find the camel standing at their doorstep with the shiny *attoush*. Lalla looked out at them with a smile and waved her hands. They were all very happy. They welcomed her and made a great feast in her honor. Their dwelling became a paradise once again. They all gathered around her. "Now," they said, "never answer the door to anyone! Never go out! We cannot afford losing you again!"

Seven Daughters and Seven Sons
[10]

LONG, LONG AGO there were two brothers who lived in separate houses but shared the farm they had inherited from their father. Each had a large family of his own. Aroush was blessed with seven sons, while Haroun had seven daughters. In a community where men dominated, the one with sons always had advantages over the other. When the two would meet in a gathering with the other neighbors, Aroush would address his brother with an air of superiority and arrogance. "Eh, get out of the center!" he would say. "I'm the father of seven virtues; you're the father of seven sins!" On each occasion Haroun was publicly humiliated and went home feeling downhearted.

One day Haroun could not stand the insults and humiliation anymore. He abandoned an important meeting of the tribe and returned home, crying like a child.

His youngest daughter ran to him, held his head in her arms, and started kissing him. "Dear Father," she cried, "what's the matter? Please, tell me."

He gently pushed her away, but she kept kissing him and insisting until he opened his heart to her. She tried to comfort him, and that made him feel better.

That night it happened to be the two brothers' turn to go out and irrigate the field of maize they shared. Haroun was getting ready to go out to meet his brother and do the work. The youngest daughter had been carefully working out a plan in her mind. She approached her father. "O Father," she said, "you look exhausted. Why not have a rest tonight and let me do the job for you?"

Her father looked at her in surprise. "But how can you, my daughter?" he asked. "Only men can go out at night and do such hard work."

She held her ground. "Father," she went on defiantly, "I'm not as weak as you think. Tell my uncle to send one of his brave sons to meet me in the field."

He looked at her again and saw her teeth clenched and red sparks shooting from her eyes.

So, Haroun went out and looked for his brother. "I'm feeling tired tonight," he said. "I'm going to send you my daughter. Ask one of your sons to meet her in the field."

His brother started laughing at the idea, but then the daughter suddenly materialized from the darkness and addressed him in an unfamiliar tone. "Uncle, there's no need to laugh that way," she said. "Send your son with me, and I'll show you what a woman can do."

Her uncle felt provoked and rushed to his son. "Come on, boy," he urged. "Take these tools and go with your cousin to the field of maize. Show her what you are! Be a man!"

The two brothers went back home to sleep, while the boy and girl disappeared. The girl was in a playful mood. When they reached the field, she said, "Look at that beautiful full moon. Let us enjoy it first and sit down here in the middle of this beautiful field. We'll have plenty of time to do the work afterward."

The boy liked the idea. For him it was like a dream to lie on the cool grass and contemplate the moon in the company of his beautiful cousin.

"It's a long night," she said, "and there is enough time for everything. Tell me some stories, my dear cousin. I like stories."

"Stories are for women. You should be full of them."

"You are right! It's our job to tell tales, and yours to listen to them."

Then she started telling him story after story, all of them sweet, until he fell asleep. When he started snoring, she left him quietly and irrigated her father's part of the field. Just as she finished, dawn was breaking and the moon had gone down. She washed her hands and feet in the stream, soaked her headscarf in the water, and walked over to her cousin. She stood behind him and started waving it around, showering him in cold water. "Hurry up, hurry up!" she shouted. "There's a storm. Let's run home."

Leaping up, he started to run, while she followed behind, still waving the headscarf and shouting, "A storm! A storm!"

When they returned home, the boy was already soaked and shivering with cold. He went straight to his bed and fell asleep, while his cousin went quietly home and rested.

Next morning, when the sun rose, the two brothers went out to check the field. The part of Haroun was irrigated, while Aroush's was still dry. The father of sons was furious. He went straight to his son and shook him awake. "Why didn't you irrigate our part of the field?" he asked angrily.

"We didn't have to irrigate it. It was raining."

"Raining? You idiot! And you're supposed to be a man! Your cousin deceived you. Oh, the guile of women!"

The son now realized that his cousin had played a trick on him. "All right," he told his father. "She may think she's clever, but tell her to do some trading with me."

So the two brothers got together again and discussed the idea. The father of daughters was not sure, because trade involved adventure and many risks. Even so, he went home and proposed the idea to his youngest daughter. She immediately took up the challenge. The following morning the two cousins mounted their camels and started their journey.

When they reached two roads that branched off, one black and one white, they stopped to think of what to do next.

"Shall we take the same road?" the boy asked.

"No," said the girl, "it's better for each of us to go his own way. When we've finished our business, we'll meet here at this same spot. Whoever arrives first should wait for the other."

"All right. Now which road do you want to take?"

"You go first. Choose whichever one you like."

The boy chose the white road.

After saying farewell, each went off in a different direction. After many days of travel, the girl reached a strange territory where houses were not like human dwellings but instead looked like large holes. She saw no human beings around, so she hid behind some thick trees and waited. When the sun set, she saw strange creatures entering their holes; then she realized she was in the territory of ghouls.

Meanwhile, her cousin found himself in a safe territory where people were hospitable and helpful. He asked about the market, and they showed him where it was. He looked around for some convenient merchandise and bought a sack of dry pomegranate skins.

Next morning the girl was surprised in her hiding place by an old woman. "What are you doing in this dangerous land?" the woman asked. "What has brought you here?"

The girl told her the whole story, and the old woman sympathized with her. She took the girl to her hut that was near the ghouls' dwelling. She taught her a lot about the life and behavior of such dangerous creatures. When the ghouls arrived home, the girl heard them talking to the door: "Open, Kzimra, with the help of God!"

The door opened automatically, and they went in. When they

were leaving in the morning, they said: "Close, Kzimra, with the help of God!" and the door shut behind them.

When the ghouls went out hunting, the girl went up to the door and spoke the same words, and the door opened. She slipped in and filled a sack full of gold and precious jewelry. Then she ordered the door to shut, and departed safe and sound. She mounted her camel and went away to meet her cousin who was already waiting for her impatiently at the crossroads.

He started laughing as he saw her carrying just a small sack.

She asked first, "What did you buy?"

"Dry pomegranate skins and a present for each member of my family," he answered with pride.

"What presents?"

"A drum for everyone. And what did you buy?"

"Just a few henna leaves."

"That's only good for women!" he said with a cackle.

So they returned home; most of the time the boy talked loudly while the girl remained silent. It was late at night when they arrived. Exhausted after the long journey, they went straight to bed and slept the whole night.

In the morning the boy's family was the first to get up. They were making a lot of noise beating their drums and celebrating, while the house of the girl was still very quiet.

When the two brothers met after breakfast, the father of sons asked, "What did your daughter buy?"

"Just a handful of henna leaves."

Aroush walked around the neighborhood with his head up, whereas Haroun kept a low profile.

Later in the day, the daughter sent her mother to borrow the scale (*moud*) from her aunt to measure the henna. When she had finished, she put a handful of gold in the bottom of the *moud*. The mother did not want to reveal the secret, but her daughter insisted. "Let them know!" she said. "This is the only way we can silence their drums and shut their mouths!"

When her mother returned the *moud* and the aunt discovered

the gold, she ran and told her husband. He felt ashamed and summoned his son. "Look, stupid boy!" he chided him. "Your cousin has brought home gold, and all you brought me was pomegranate skins. You're not a man."

Suddenly, the drums stopped beating, and the celebration turned into rage and envy. The son was deeply hurt and once again challenged his cousin. "If she's woman enough," he told his father, "tell her to give me one more chance!"

When his cousin heard of the new challenge, she pretended to refuse to take it up. But her father was very enthusiastic and urged her to go on.

"All right," she said. "I'm ready. Tell my uncle I'll meet his son tomorrow."

The following day the two cousins took to the road again. They arrived at the same crossroads.

"This time," the boy said, "I'll take the black road, and you take the white one."

"Just as you wish, my dear cousin," the girl replied in a subdued tone.

After some distance the girl took a detour and went in the direction of the ghouls' territory. She followed the same path she had taken before and filled two sacks of gold; in no time she had returned to the crossroads and waited for her cousin to join her.

Meanwhile, the boy found himself in an unfamiliar territory. He saw something like a house and went to ask where he could find the market. Two large ghouls opened the door. "What do you want, boy?" they demanded.

When the boy saw them, he was paralyzed by fear and could not even speak.

"Speak up, boy!" they said. "Or else we'll eat you and your camel."

He made an effort to answer. "My father has sent me to bring him some gold," he blurted out.

They laughed. "We'll give you something better than gold," they replied with a laugh. "Give us your bags, and we'll fill them with olive oil. Just wait there."

They went in and shut themselves inside the two bags. "Come in and pick up your bags," they shouted.

He lifted his two bags, fixed them on his camel and went away very happy. The bags were so heavy that the camel could hardly move.

He found his cousin waiting for him at their meeting place. "What did you buy this time?" he asked her.

"Pomegranate skins. And what about you?"

"Olive oil!"

She felt the bags with her fingers and realized what was in them, but kept quiet all the way back home. She was scared the strange creatures would tear the bags open and devour them. She was visibly pale and trembling, while he was in a triumphant mood, imagining that she was burning with jealousy.

As soon as they got home, his father asked, "What is it this time?"

"Two skins full of olive oil!"

They took the two heavy skins inside the house and placed them in the food store where the servant worked and slept.

Next day the servant was grinding wheat in the stone mill and singing to herself. She remembered the oil and thought of stealing a few drops to put on her disheveled hair. She found a needle and pricked the bag where the skin was hidden. She waited, but no oil came out. Instead, something strange started moving around inside the bag. She tried the other bag and noticed the same movement, just like waves. After a moment's thought she guessed what was inside and was overcome by terror. Her legs failed her, so she could not get out of the room. She resumed her grinding and started singing a different song with chattering teeth: "Oh, my dear lady," she sang, "your son has brought home those who will devour us and our neighbors."

Her sad song attracted her mistress. She understood the message and ran to tell her husband. He came to the servant's door and motioned to her to come out very quietly. When the servant saw him, she finally had the courage to leave the room. The father then ordered complete silence. Quickly digging a *metmoura*, he collected a lot of wood near it. Then he called for his son and put his finger on his mouth, warning him not to talk. They dragged the two bags and lowered them carefully into the pit, then he pushed his son in after them. Once he had filled the *metmoura* with wood, he set the whole thing on fire.

"Now, my son," he shouted, "bathe and fry in the oil you brought me!"

The smoke attracted the neighbors, who were afraid it was a fire. They congregated by the house of the father of seven sons. It was the servant who revealed the whole story to them.

Lunja

[11]

LUNJA WAS A GIRL of stunning beauty, and she was an only child. Ever since her birth she had been kept indoors and was never allowed to see the world outside.

One day, when her father and mother went away to work in the fields, she opened the door and walked outside. Suddenly, five beautiful birds landed right in front of her. They were such fascinating creatures that she could not take her eyes off them. They looked up at her with pitiful eyes, as though begging for food. In fact, they did look very hungry. She went into the house and brought them some wheat grains, but they refused to eat. She tried other sorts of seeds, but still they just stared at her. She thought of her mother's jewels and precious stones. She found them and gave them to the birds, who immediately devoured them. When she had emptied the box, the birds flew away, but not very far.

As soon as she realized the mistake she had made, she went after them, hoping to get her mother's treasure back. The birds kept appearing and disappearing, luring her farther and farther away. When she was very tired and lost, she stopped and started crying. The birds came back. "Do you want to go back home," they asked, "or do you want to go with us?"

She hesitated.

"It's dangerous to go with us," the birds cautioned. "Our mother is a ghoul."

"Let the river that took you take me," Lunja replied. And she followed them wherever they went.

After many days and nights, they told her, "Now we're very close to our mother."

"Let the river that took you take me," she said once again.

They reached a cavern. At its entrance the birds spoke to her again. "Now we'll go in," they said. "Our mother is usually grinding grain, laying one breast on her right and another on the left, her breasts being too long and flabby. Once you're inside the cavern, you'll first encounter a needle. You must tell her: 'May God make your eye large enough for me to get through.' When you get through, you should take one breast and suck at it. We shall distract our mother until you've sucked from both breasts."

Lunja followed their instructions carefully. When she finished sucking from both breasts, the mother ghoul became aware of her presence. She turned on her children. "Ah! I see," she said. "It must have been Aissa and Moussa who told you what to do. Now that you've sucked my milk, I can't eat you. But for the milk you now share with Aissa and Moussa, I'd have sucked your blood in a single drop, eaten your flesh in one swallow, and cast your bones to the seven skies. But now you'll stay with me forever."

Every day the ghoul went out hunting and brought Lunja the best food. "Eat whatever you desire," she said, "but you'll be my eternal companion."

In a remote land her cousin, the son of a sultan, used to play games with other children. He could beat them at any game, so they became resentful and started conspiring among themselves. They gathered at the edge of the playground just beside an old woman's hut. She overheard them and decided to help. She came out of her hut. "I'm well aware of that boy's arrogance," she whispered to them. "I can help you defeat him. Listen, I'll be inside steaming couscous. You entice him to play with the ball near my hut. One of you will kick the ball inside. Let him come to retrieve it."

They did exactly what she told them and waited for her plan to take effect. The sultan's son ran into her hut without asking permission. "Who do you think you are?" she yelled at him. "You've ruined my couscous. How dare you?"

She chased him out of the hut, showering him with insults in front of the other boys. "How dare you do this to such a poor and weak woman?" she yelled. "You think you're a man? And you've left your cousin Lunja a captive in the country of ghouls! Shame upon you!"

The boy felt hurt and humiliated in front of the other boys. He went to see his mother, trembling and feverish. He told her what the old woman had said to him. Then he asked his mother to cook a very hot soup and invite the woman. She did so. When the woman came in and started eating, the boy jumped and held her hand in the bowl. "Now," he demanded, "tell me all about Lunja my cousin, or I won't release your hand."

The woman begged him to let go of her hand and promised to tell him everything. She sat down and told him the whole tale and the whereabouts of his cousin. Then he let her go.

Very early the next morning he prepared his white horse, brought his white-and-black greyhound with him, and set off in search of his cousin. He traveled farther and farther, with the greyhound following behind. When he entered a strange territory (just as the old woman had described it for him), he rested for a while beside a spring in order to reflect on his next move. An old woman who had come to collect water found him there. "Oh, handsome boy," she asked, "what has brought you to this dangerous country of ghouls?"

He told her what he was looking for. She felt sorry for him and invited him back to her house to eat and sleep. Next morning she told him, "Now then, you stay here. I'll go around to see what I can find out."

When she returned she told him about the cavern where Lunja was held captive and what the ghoul was doing with her. Every night the ghoul gave Lunja her hair to plait, and next morning she had to unplait it and count the hairs one by one.

For many days the old woman hovered around the ghoul's cavern, spying and reporting to the young man what she heard and saw. Meanwhile, she was trying to think of a stratagem to help him save his cousin.

One day the old woman told the young man, "Go to the market and buy me some fat."

He carried out her request. The following day she waited until the ghoul left the cavern, then slipped in and talked to Lunja. "Come with me quickly," she said. "Your cousin's waiting for you."

Lunja went out with the old woman to meet her cousin. He told her why he had come and begged her to go back with him. But Lunja replied that it was impossible; the ghoul would return at night and chase after them. The old woman was listening to their conversation. "No, no," she interrupted. "Not now. The plan's not yet developed enough for you to leave."

She asked Lunja for details about the life and behavior of the ghoul: how she slept, when she woke up, and when she went out. Lunja gave her all these details. "And," she added, "there are other secrets she's never shared with me."

"Get as much information as you can," the old woman counseled. "Do your best. I need to know more in order to perfect my plans for a safe escape."

After this brief encounter with her cousin, Lunja went back into the cavern.

That night the ghoul came home, and Lunja treated her with great affection and humor. The ghoul was pleased.

"Look," Lunja commented casually, "we've been living together for a long time, but you still don't trust me. I'm unhappy.

You know I love you, but you won't tell me everything about your life."

So the ghoul opened up her heart to her and revealed more secrets to her.

Next day Lunja counted the ghoul's hair and found one missing. Thereafter, every day she noticed one hair less.

Lunja regularly reported new information to the old woman. When many days had passed, the boy said, "So, now we can escape."

"The plan's not ready yet," the woman replied. "Be patient and wait until I tell you."

Day after day he waited anxiously, and the old woman kept prolonging his stay until she felt he was losing his mind. Then she asked him to go to the market again and buy her some henna. That he did, hoping it would be her last request.

The old woman took the henna leaves to Lunja and instructed her to crush them in a *mehras*, a mortar, until they became a thin powder. Another day she told her to mix the powder with water and use it to paint everything in the cavern and all utensils in the kitchen. It took Lunja a few more days to do that. When she had finished, she checked again to make sure that everything had its share of henna. The only object she did not paint with henna was the *mehras* itself, but she knew there was enough henna sticking to it since she had used it to crush the leaves.

Now the plan was ready for the two cousins to escape. The old woman finally allowed them to set off while the ghoul was sleeping. They mounted the white horse and rode away with the greyhound following them.

The *mehras* looked around and noticed that everything in the house was painted with henna except itself. It was jealous and started knocking. "Wake up! Wake up!" it yelled. "Her cousin has taken her away!"

The ghoul leaped up from her lair and realized that Lunja was missing. She felt betrayed and became furious. She went out and started following their scent. "Where are you, Lunja?" she howled. "You daughter of a betrayer! Where are you?"

After running for miles she finally caught sight of them. "Lunja, betrayer's daughter!" she yelled. "Wait for me!"

But they spurred the horse and continued to race away. The ghoul ran after them like mad, never losing sight of the white horse. When the race became a challenge for her, she addressed Lunja again. "What does your cousin eat," she asked, "in order not to get tired?"

Lunja turned around. "Wood and grass," she replied.

The ghoul started devouring wood and grass, but she still could not close the gap. Again she asked, "What does the horse eat?"

"It eats its own knees," Lunja replied.

The ghoul chewed her knees and collapsed. When she realized she no longer had any strength left, she called out to Lunja to stop and listen to her last piece of advice. Lunja begged her cousin to stop.

"On your way home," the ghoul said, "you'll come across two roads, one red and one white. Follow the red one. You'll come to two springs, one clean and one muddy. Drink from the unclean one. If you make a mistake, you'll come across a huge white bird. He will issue an invitation to you. When he offers you food, eat one mouthful and drop one in your lap. When you've finished, he'll ask you to drop what you ate."

Lunja and her cousin rode away, leaving the ghoul dying. After many miles they reached the two roads.

"Let's follow the ghoul's advice," Lunja told her cousin.

He laughed mockingly and insisted on taking the white road. Later, they found the two springs as the ghoul had described. Again the cousin dismissed the ghoul's warning and drank from the clean spring, but Lunja drank from the muddy one. They resumed their journey, and after a while the white bird did indeed meet them. He invited them to eat, and Lunja reminded her cousin to eat one mouthful and drop one in his lap. But he was very hungry and ate everything, while she dropped a few mouthfuls in her lap. When the meal was finished, the white bird said, "Now, drop what you've eaten."

Lunja stood up and let down what she had saved, but her cousin had nothing to show.

The white bird now ordered him to remount his horse, then swallowed him up along with the horse and everything and flew away into the sky.

Lunja and the greyhound were now left alone. They continued on their way until they reached a valley. There Lunja slew the greyhound, dried its skin in the sun and wind, and put it on. She walked on in disguise until she reached the territory of her uncle, the sultan. Disguised as a greyhound, Lunja walked to the entrance of the palace and took a rest. When the sultan saw her, he guessed his son was lost forever. He instructed his slaves to take care of the greyhound by making her a kennel outside the palace and giving her bran mixed with water to eat.

A few days later the white bird appeared in the sky and flew close to the greyhound's head. From his stomach a voice emerged addressing Lunja: "O Lunja!" it cried.

"Yes, dear cousin," she answered.

"What have you eaten?"

"Bran mixed in water."

"Where did you sleep?"

"Outside."

"Cursed be my father and mother who neglect you and treat you like a dog."

Then he disappeared into the sky. Every day the same dialogue was repeated. One day a beggar happened to be passing by and overheard the conversation. He asked to see the sultan because he had a secret to reveal to him. The sultan agreed to grant him an audience. That same day the sultan gave the greyhound *terid*, a special meal, brought her inside the palace, and gave her a comfortable bed. Next morning he took her out and concealed himself nearby, waiting for the bird to arrive. When the white bird came and hovered over the greyhound, the sultan listened to their conversation:

"O dear Lunja! What have you eaten?"

"O dear cousin, they gave me *terid*."

"And where did you sleep?"

"Inside the palace in a comfortable bed."

"God bless my father and mother."

At that the sultan suddenly cried out. "O my beloved son," he said, "what must I do to have you back?"

The voice from the bird's belly addressed the greyhound. "Tell my father," it said, "to slay a black bull and make a big meal for the birds. Then, once the white bird has eaten a lot, tell Father to ask him to drop what he has eaten."

The sultan got the message. On the following day he had a large meal ready. The flock of birds arrived, the white one among them. They landed and started eating until they had consumed everything. The white bird was the one that had eaten the most, so much that it could not fly.

The sultan approached the bird. "Now, drop what you've eaten," he said.

"Do you want him blind?" the bird asked.

"No."

"Do you want him crippled?"

"No. I want him back exactly as he was, on his white horse."

The sultan waited very anxiously for a while. Suddenly, his son emerged from the bird's belly on the back of the white horse. The father was overwhelmed with joy. The son dismounted, walked straight over to the greyhound, and kissed her very affectionately. Then he turned and embraced his father. The sultan ordered his town crier to announce his son's homecoming. A big celebration began. The mother came running out and hugged her son, shedding tears of joy.

Throughout the celebration the son kept the greyhound by his side, caressing her and giving her the best food.

When night came, he decided to keep the greyhound with him in his bedroom. He asked a slave to bring him some hot water. Everyone went happily to bed, but they wondered what he was doing with the greyhound and the hot water.

In the morning they woke up early, and a splendid breakfast was prepared. The sultan and his wife sent a slave to their son's chamber with a tray full of food. No sooner had the slave knocked and opened the door than she let the tray fall from her hands and uttered a loud scream. The sultan and his wife rushed to the scene. They saw the slave still frozen with astonishment, her hands empty.

"What is it?" they asked.

"The moon, the moon!" she said. "I've seen the moon in your son's bedroom. Oh, my lord, I have never seen such beauty!"

At that the son emerged holding Lunja by her arm. He introduced her to his father and mother: "This is Lunja, my cousin," he said. "I have saved her from the country of ghouls."

He kissed her in front of everyone, tears filling his eyes. So it was that they had a big wedding and lived happily ever after.

Hdiddan

[12]

THERE ONCE WAS a couple who had seven sons. They lived a life of poverty. One day the father had an idea: he would emigrate to another country to find work. They all departed. After many miles of travel, the children began to feel tired and refused to walk any farther. The first son asked his father to make him a house of wood. He stayed there, and the others resumed their journey. Then the second son asked his father for the same thing, so he built him a house, too. The other children followed suit until only one was left. The family, by now reduced to just father, mother, and the seventh son whose name was Hdiddan, walked on and on until his one remaining son could no longer walk. He stopped. "Father," he asked, "build me a house of iron. I shall stay here."

The father did his best, and he and the mother were left to proceed on their journey alone.

The ghouls were tracking them. They ate the sons one after the other until they reached the last one who was hiding inside an iron house. They tried to break in but failed. When the ghouls despaired, they went to live in the nearby forest, except for their old, half-blind sister called Mamma Ghoula and her ugly daughter. They waited around for Hdiddan to come out, so they could eat him.

One day she went over to the iron house. "Hdiddan!" she yelled. "We're neighbors. You've nothing to fear. Let's go together and collect some fruit in the nearby forest."

"My basket is torn," came the reply from inside. "I'm repairing it, Mamma Ghoula. Wait for me."

The half-blind Ghoula returned to her hut and waited. Meanwhile, Hdiddan went out to the forest and brought back some fruit. When Mamma Ghoula and her daughter went to the trees, they found no fruit.

She tried again. "Hdiddan," she shouted, "let's go and bring water from the spring."

"My water skin's torn. I have to repair it first. Wait for me."

She went back to her hut and waited for a long time. When he did not appear, she went with her daughter to the spring and found the water muddied and full of dirt. "So," she told her daughter, "it must be the wicked Hdiddan who has done it."

Mamma Ghoula thought up all sorts of tricks to trap Hdiddan, but he always outwitted her. In fact, he started laughing at her and making her life unbearable. So, she wondered, what trick would get rid of him?

She went to see an old man who was renowned for his cunning. "What can I do," she asked, "to catch Hdiddan?"

"You must find an old man and get his brain. Paint it on the back of Hdiddan's donkey. He'll get glued to it, then it'll be easy to catch him."

Mamma Ghoula thought for a minute. "You're the nearest," she said.

She killed the old man and took his brain. She painted the back of Hdiddan's donkey and waited for him to go out to the spring. When Hdiddan got stuck, Mamma Ghoula surprised him and finally managed to catch him.

"Please don't eat me now," he begged her. "You can see how thin I am. Give me time to get fat."

"I won't let you go!"

"That's not what I mean. If you want to find enough flesh on me, shut me in a jar of dates and put a pestle in with me. I'll knock on the jar when I have finished the dates."

When he had become strong, he knocked on the jar with the pestle.

"Now," she said, "I'm going to eat you."

"But there is too much fat in me. Why don't you invite your brothers?"

She liked the idea and called her daughter. She told her to keep an eye on him until she returned with her brothers.

When the Ghoula went into the forest searching for her brothers, Hdiddan was left alone with her daughter. They started talking.

"My mother's asked me to make a meal of you," she said.

The man started telling her nice stories, full of weddings and married bliss. Then he told her how beautiful she was, except that her hair was disheveled and kept falling over her beautiful face. It needed cutting. She said she had no knife and could not manage it with her awkward claws. He immediately offered to help so that everyone would be very jealous of her.

When she came over to him, he grabbed her hair and slit her throat. He took off her skin and put it on. He quickly cut her up into pieces and cooked her in a big pot. When the Ghoula returned with her brothers, Hdiddan shouted to them in a faked voice, "You are very welcome for dinner, Mother and uncles."

He offered them a large plate full of meat. "Mamma," he said, "now that Hdiddan is dead, give me the key to his hut."

She handed it to him, and he walked out. Outside he started collecting wood and singing, "Mamma Ghoula's eating her own daughter!"

She heard what he said. "Catch him immediately!" she ordered her brothers. They charged out to look for him.

"Come and catch me," he shouted at them. "I'm under the pile of firewood."

They all jumped on the pile and fell in a trap. He then set the pile of wood on fire and burned them all. He ran off, laughing at the half-blind, old Ghoula.

A Tale of Two Women

[13]

LONG, LONG AGO there were two close neighbors who both happened to be widows. All they inherited from their husbands was a large number of young children. One of them was named Good-Intentions and the other Bad-Intentions. They used to meet and talk about their hardships and the sufferings of their children. One day they decided to travel in search of food and money. They discussed a few arrangements regarding their shared journey. When they had agreed on every detail, they took an oath of trust never to betray each other and to support each other in all circumstances.

That settled, they each provided some food to take with them on their journey, the duration of which they could not determine. Thus, they entrusted their children to God's protection and departed.

Day and night they walked. For the first two days they had no rest and ate no food. However, on the third day, Good-Intentions started to feel weak and hungry. She stopped and said to her companion, "Oh, I'm starving. Now, whose food shall we start with, yours or mine?"

Her companion said, "Let's begin by yours first. It's the same anyway. When we finish it, we'll eat mine."

So, they settled down by the road and ate, then they resumed their journey.

Two days went by. Once again Good-Intentions felt hungry, but the other was fit and showed no sign of hunger or tiredness at all. Good-Intentions was ashamed of herself, but she could not resist the pain in her stomach. She asked Bad-Intentions to have a rest and eat something. They ate what was left of Good-Intentions's food. Then they walked on, resting only for an hour or two to get some sleep.

Three days later Good-Intentions again started to suffer from hunger, but she was embarrassed to ask for food. When her legs started giving away, she collapsed.

"What's wrong with you?" her companion asked.

"Oh, my friend, I'm dying of hunger. Can we have something to eat?"

"Do you still have any left?"

"We finished mine. Let's have yours."

"Mine! We still have a long way to go. I can't give you my food."

"But we agreed to share. I gave you mine during the first days, didn't I?"

Bad-Intentions did not want to waste any more time, so she told her point-blank, "Give me one of your eyes, and I'll give you food."

Good-Intentions now realized the betrayal of trust, but she had no energy to argue. She begged her companion and cried until she lost her voice. Bad-Intentions heartlessly repeated her condition. When Good-Intentions was going mad with hunger, she accepted the terms. Plucking out one of her eyes, she handed it to her companion. They resumed their walk, but by now on very bad terms.

Bad-Intentions never complained of hunger because she was secretly sneaking food from her bag. After a few more miles, Good-Intentions once again stopped and begged her for food.

Bad-Intentions asked her for her second eye, and she gave it to her in exchange for a small morsel.

Now that Good-Intentions was completely blind, she could no longer walk. Bad-Intentions finally abandoned her in a forest and went on by herself. When night fell, the deceived and blind woman tried to fall asleep, but she was scared by the sound of wild animals howling and growling all around her. She groped her way toward a tree and climbed it in order to hide among the branches. But the beasts were attracted by her scent and gathered under her hiding place. They started debating among themselves what to do to get her down. But one of them said, "Listen, brothers, there is nothing up there. Let's go and look elsewhere."

"In any case," another pointed out, "this tree is sacred and very useful. Its leaves cure blindness. If you rub a leaf on your blind eye, it'll immediately regain its sight."

The woman was listening closely to their discussion, her feelings changing from fear to intense curiosity. Then the animals left.

Exhausted and anxious, Good-Intentions fell asleep perched on a branch. When she woke up in the morning, the first thing she remembered was the power the tree had to cure blindness. She picked up a leaf and rubbed it on her right eye; it opened again. She did the same for the left eye, too, and thus recovered her vision completely. Before leaving, she collected a handful of leaves, wrapped them up in her headscarf and continued her journey. She looked for a few eggs and some grass and ate them to give her energy. Thus, she went on her way, happy that her sight was restored.

After a few days she came to a territory where she found people. She started begging for food. People were hospitable and kind to her. One day she heard a few women talking about their sultan. She understood that he was suffering from blindness; he would pay anything for a cure. She inquired about the whereabouts of the palace, and they showed her. At the gate the guards stopped her and told her to beg somewhere else. She explained to them that she had come to offer the sultan some help. The guards discussed the matter among themselves, then sent a messenger to inform the sultan of the presence of a beggar woman, a stranger, who wanted to see him. In his desperate straits he was willing to receive anyone. He allowed his messenger to bring her to him.

When he received her, he immediately asked, "Old woman, what help do you have to give me? Speak."

"With the help of God," she replied, "I've come to cure you of your blindness. But I want to be alone with you."

He gestured to his guards to leave them alone. "Come close," he said, "and show me what you can do."

She untied her headscarf and took out the leaves. She rubbed one on his eye. After a short while, it was open.

"And now the other one, please," he said.

She did the same thing, and with both eyes he was able to see an old, dirty woman kneeling in front of him.

"Come and take a seat beside me," he said. "Don't kneel. You are a great woman. With God's help, I shall make you rich."

His joy knew no bounds. He immediately called his family and advisers and gave them the good news. The palace was soon dancing with happiness. The news also got to the people, who started celebrating.

The sultan instructed his maids to take care of the woman. They gave her a royal bath and dressed her in the best clothes they had. A big banquet was given in the old woman's honor to which the royal family and dignitaries were invited. The sultan sat beside the old woman. After the banquet, the sultan invited her to stay in his palace as long as she liked. But she told him she had to go back home where her poor children were waiting for her to feed them.

Next day he gave her a lot of gold and asked her to come back for more whenever she wished. He sent with her two horsemen to accompany her as far as she wanted. When she reached the frontiers of her homeland, she thanked them and continued home, where she found her children waiting for her. She asked them if their neighbor, Bad-Intentions, had returned home, but as yet there was no sign of her.

Soon her children became rich and ate very well. The children of Bad-Intentions noticed the change and came to ask for help. Good-Intentions pitied them and gave them enough gold.

Months later, Bad-Intentions finally showed up, looking older, dirty, and emaciated. She was surprised to find her companion had arrived and with her sight restored. Her children also told her that Good-Intentions had brought a lot of gold and how kind she was to them. But she merely kept quiet, looking miserable.

One day she came to visit Good-Intentions and apologized to her. Good-Intentions had no grudge against her. In fact, Bad-Intentions's real purpose was to know how she got hold of so much gold. Good-Intentions told her the whole story.

A few days later Bad-Intentions departed on the same journey without informing her neighbor. She found the tree where she had abandoned her companion, blind and in utter despair. When night fell, Bad-Intentions climbed the tree to escape from wild beasts. They smelled her scent and again congregated around the tree.

"I'll go up there," said a huge snake, "and find out for you."

The snake found Bad-Intentions perching on a branch and flung her down to the animals. They were grabbing her before she even reached the ground. When a long time had passed and she did not reappear, her children lost all hope of seeing her again.

Thus it was that Good-Intentions invited them to live with her children and treated them all with the same loving care.

Aamar and His Sister

[14]

A COUPLE HAD two children, a son and a daughter. When the wife died, the father took care of the young children. But he found it difficult to raise them, so he married another woman to help him with the task. However, the stepmother hated the children and started planning to get rid of them.

One night she made couscous with chicken. When dinner was ready, she took the children to the kitchen and gave them an empty plate and two spoons. The father arrived and asked her to feed the children, but she said they had already had their dinner. When the children were tired, they fell asleep.

Next morning, the woman broke utensils and blamed the children. She complained to her husband. Angry, he took the children to a forest. "Wait for me here," he said. "I'll be back."

Night came, but still the father did not come back. The daughter, who was the older child, realized that their father had given them up. "Let's look for a shelter," she suggested to her brother.

They walked around. Seeing a light in the distance they walked toward it, believing it to come from a bushman's hut. When they got there, they discovered an abandoned house, but they did not know who had lit the fire. They adopted the house as their home and settled in there. The boy made traps for birds and rabbits, and his sister cooked them.

One day the sister went out into the forest and was looking around while her brother was away trying to catch birds. She saw a strange animal going into a hole and followed it. Thrusting her hand in the hole she tried to pull the animal out, but it had gone in very deep. So she dug in, too; eventually, her fingers touched an object. She started feeling it and came upon a handle. She drew it out. It was so heavy that she started sweating. Suddenly, the object popped out; it was an old jar. She opened it and found it full of gold and silver. She buried it in a secret place and did not tell her brother. She waited a couple of years, then one day she raised the subject. "Just suppose," she said, "that I found a lot of gold and silver. What would you do with it?"

"I'd buy a lot of toys to play with," he replied.

She realized that he was still a child; she would wait for him to grow up. Time passed, and on another day she asked him the same question.

"I'd buy a gun," he replied, "and shoot Father and his wife."

She was still not satisfied and had to wait still more years. At last he gave her a different answer.

"I'd buy some cattle," he said, "and turn this old house into a real home for us to live in."

She was happy with his answer and showed him the jar. He bought cattle and repaired the house. He was now a mature man.

One night, as brother and sister were sitting and talking happily, they heard a knock at the door. The brother opened and found a woman traveler. She asked for food and shelter, and he welcomed her. The sister gave her some food and a comfortable bed.

Next morning the stranger expressed her wish to stay a little longer, and they had no objections. She offered to help the sister with the housework, but the latter said she did not need help. The

visitor stayed on and on until eventually the sister started to suspect that she might have some evil plan. She expressed her feelings to her brother, but all he said was: "Oh, what can she do?"

When the sister could not stand her anymore, she told her to
leave. The woman refused. "I'm going to marry Aamar," she said.

The sister was surprised. When she told her brother, he confirmed that such was his intention.

"You cannot marry this wandering woman," she told him angrily. "I'll find you the most beautiful girl for a wife. Send this one
packing!"

Instead, he ignored his sister's advice. Next day he married the
woman.

The two women hated each other. The wife started contriving
evil schemes against the sister. One day she killed a sheep and
blamed it on her. But the brother did not believe his wife. Another
day she killed her own babies and accused the sister. Still Aamar
did not believe her. On the third attempt she succeeded. She
brought three snake eggs. "Now," she told the sister, "if one of us
can swallow these eggs, she is the one who really loves Aamar."

To pass the test the sister pounced on the eggs and swallowed
them.

A few days later her brother started to notice some change in
his sister. Meanwhile, his wife dropped a few indirect hints to in-
flame his suspicions. The sister's belly began to swell. Aamar believed that some journeyman had made his sister pregnant. For a
while he said nothing, but one day he tied her to a tree and cut off
her hands as a punishment. She managed to get away from the
house and eventually found refuge somewhere in a distant forest
where only deer lived. They accepted her among them.

One day the sultan was on a hunting expedition, and one of his
slaves caught a glimpse of her. He thought it was a strange creature

guarding the deer. He reported the news to the sultan, and the latter immediately ordered his soldiers to catch the creature and bring it to him.

They placed a plate of couscous and a fire in the forest to test whether it was a human being or a jinn. If it were a devil, it would run away, but if a human being it would eat and warm herself.

At night she was attracted by the fire and the smell of food and came to eat and keep herself warm. She was caught and taken to the sultan. She told him her story. He summoned an old woman who examined her and understood her problem. The old woman asked for a sheep to be slaughtered, then roasted it with too much salt. She made her eat too much until she started crying out for water. They tied her by her feet to a tree and placed a bowl of water under her mouth. Suddenly, snakes started jumping out and dropping into the bowl. When three snakes were out, she was given water to drink.

Out of pity the sultan asked her to marry him.

"How can you marry a poor, handless woman?" she asked in amazement.

Nevertheless, the sultan married her and gave her many slaves to serve her.

When he was getting ready to go away on a mission, he advised her not to talk or deal with his two other wives. However, while he was away, the wives tempted her to join them in the garden to tell stories and jokes. On her way to meet them, she fell in a deep dry well. There she gave birth to twins. The two wives closed up the well as though they knew nothing. When the sultan came home, he was told she had escaped.

Then one day, as a slave was passing by, he overheard her singing to her babies. He was frightened by a voice coming from underground. He opened up the well. "Are you a human being or a jinn?" he asked.

"A human being," she replied, "and the third wife of the sultan."

The slave helped her out and took her back to her apartment. The two other wives were afraid that if she told the sultan what

they had done to her, he would kill them. So they went and threatened her. "If you tell the sultan," they said, "we'll tell him that the
twins are not his offspring." Just to be safe, they demanded that she
kill the twins, but instead she left the palace with her babies.

And so she traversed the wide world. When one of her children, named Abdurrahman, was thirsty and was crying out for
water, she looked for a spring, but she could not give him the water
since she had no hands. She tried to use her feet and shoulders, but
it did not work. Suddenly, as her right arm touched the water, it
grew a hand that looked decorated with henna. The other boy,
Othman, was crying out for water, too; she tried the other arm,
and, no sooner did it brush the water than it too grew into a
healthy hand decorated with henna. She gave her children plenty
of water and continued her wanderings until she came upon a deserted house. The owners had died, leaving everything behind.
There it was that she settled down with her children.

When the sultan returned home from his mission, he discovered that she was missing. His wives told him she was bored and
had run away. He went looking for her father and asked that he
join him in searching for her. They kept roaming around the world
until they arrived where she had settled. When she saw them
climbing the hill toward her house, she recognized them. She disguised herself. When they arrived and asked her if she had not
seen a woman of such-and-such description, she said she had not.
As it was nighttime, she invited them to stay as guests. She was
very hospitable. After dinner, she gave them a large room near
hers and went to sleep with her children. She insisted that the
children ask her to tell them stories. She started telling them a
story loudly enough to be heard in the next room. The two men
listened. She was narrating her own story: "Oh, my dear sons, my
brother, Aamar, and I were living together when he married a
wicked woman. . . . I married a sultan, and you are his real sons.

. . . His wives hated me and caused me all this trouble and misery, but God will repay them . . ."

Both the sultan and her father were stunned. Her father felt so guilty that the earth started swallowing him up until only his beard was visible. Next day they took her and the children back to the palace. The sultan condemned his wives and sentenced them to be burned alive. He and his wife and children lived happily ever after.

Three Women

[15]

IN THE COUNTRYSIDE lived three single women who were the closest friends. Wherever they went, they were always seen together.

One day they went out to collect grass for cattle. Although there was grass everywhere, the field of beans attracted them most. But they were afraid of the owner who was himself an old bachelor. The women sat down by the edge of the field talking. "If the owner of this field marries me," one of them said, "I'll make him a huge loaf of bread out of one single grain."

"If he marries me," the second one said, "I'll make him a large pot of bean soup with a single bean."

"If he marries me," said the third, "I'll bear him a son with a golden birthmark on his forehead."

The man, who happened to be hidden nearby, overheard them and smiled. He decided to marry the three of them together, and they all welcomed the idea.

The first woman failed to make him the loaf of bread she had promised, and the second failed to make him the bean soup with one bean. Even so, he did not divorce them. A year later the third woman fulfilled her promise and gave birth to a son with a golden birthmark on the forehead.

The other two wives were jealous and started plotting against her. When the child was born, they cut off his little finger and thrust it in the mother's mouth while she was still exhausted after her labors. They gave the baby to a woman to bury alive. When the husband arrived, they told him she had eaten her baby. The mother, still recuperating, was shocked by the accusation and could not defend herself. When she said nothing, her husband punished her.

Far away a woman was taking care of the baby until he grew up. When he was playing with other children, one of them insulted him by saying that he was only a foundling. He returned home crying and asked the woman who he thought was his mother to tell him the truth. She was furious and denied the accusation. He complained that he was very hungry and wanted some melted butter. When the woman had melted it, he thrust her hand onto the plate and made her confess. It was then that she told him the whole story.

The following day he left her in search of his real mother and family. He bought some nice clothes, hoping that he would find his mother and give her a present. His companions during the quest were a wolf, a sheep, and a greyhound. Whenever people saw them, they would exclaim, "Glory be to God! A wolf, a sheep, and a greyhound together! And yet they don't fight each other."

"Glory be to God!" the young man would reply. "They're only animals, and yet they love each other. But a mother ate her baby!"

"We've never heard of such a woman," people would reply.

So he continued his journey, trying to get information about his missing mother. For a long time he met only with disappointment, but then he finally heard a man say, "Yes, there is such a mother. I know her."

The young man begged the man to show him where she lived. The man indicated an isolated hut. The young man walked there, followed by his companions. When that woman saw him, she too exclaimed, "Glory be to God! A wolf, a sheep, and a greyhound, all living together!"

"Glory be to God!" the young man replied. "They're only animals, and yet they love each other. But a mother ate her baby!"

The miserable woman lowered her gaze. "Yes," she admitted, "I'm that very woman."

He sat down with her and asked her how and why she had done it. She told him she could not remember the details. All she could remember was she had given birth to a beautiful son, but, when she recovered from her exhaustion, she was told she had eaten him. The only proof her husband had was the little finger stuck into her mouth. He had condemned her to wear a dog's hide, sleep in the kitchen, and watch the camels. Afterward, she was sent away to live even farther from the house in the small hut where she was now living.

After listening to her story, he asked her if he could see the man himself, so she showed him where to find him. He was invited in as a guest. When dinner was served, the young man refused to eat unless the shepherdess joined them. The husband was not happy. "How can a dirty shepherdess, a cursed woman, share food with us?" he asked.

However, the young man insisted, and finally the husband gave in reluctantly. When the man summoned her to dinner, she was confused by such a sudden change. When dinner was over, the guest asked the man for some hot water and soap for his ablutions. He gave the water and the soap to the shepherdess and asked her to wash herself. He also gave her the bag he was carrying with him. "Change into these clothes," he told her.

Next morning everybody was surprised to see a clean and beautiful woman dressed in new clothes.

It was then that the guest asked the man why he had punished that woman. The husband gave him his reasons. The guest asked for proof, but the man was not quite sure. "That's what my wives told me," he said, "and only God knows the whole truth."

"Just suppose your son never really died." the guest said. "Would you be able to recognize him?"

"Although I never had a chance to see him, I do know for sure he has a golden birthmark on his forehead."

The shepherdess was asked the same question and gave the same reply.

Next night the three of them were having dinner together in a large room. Suddenly, the guest said, "Blow out the candle for a moment."

It was very dark. The guest took off his turban, and suddenly the golden birthmark on his forehead lighted up the room. The mother and father jumped up from their corners, hugged him, and wept tears of joy for a long time. Thus, the truth was finally revealed.

Immediately, the man called his other two wives and made them confess. When they did, he condemned them to wear dogs' hides, to eat with dogs, and sleep outside. After some time, they were tied to a horse and dragged in front of everyone for a long distance until they died. Afterward, father, mother, and son lived happily ever after.

Nunja and the White Dove

[16]

THERE WAS ONCE a man who had two wives and was happy with both. The first one gave him a son and a daughter named Nunja, and the second only a daughter named Aakasha. The wives went out to help irrigate the field. One day they were admiring a tapestry of green grass.

"How I wish I were a cow," the first wife said, "so I could eat all this grass."

"Do you really want to become a cow?" the second wife asked.

The other was indeed serious, so the second wife struck her with her necklace; immediately, she turned into a cow and started eating the grass. When she had had her fill, she started mooing to express her desire to be turned back into a woman. But the other wife refused to strike her with the necklace again. Instead, she returned home, and the cow followed her, mooing all the way.

The brother and sister went out looking for their mother, but the second wife simply pointed at a cow. "Your mother's turned into a cow," she said.

The cow kept mooing and making a huge fuss. The wife got annoyed and asked her husband to slaughter her. He agreed. All they kept was the head and a bit of the meat, and they distributed the rest to their neighbors. After eating the meat, the wife collected the bones and buried them near the house.

The two children saw where the bones were buried. After their mother's disappearance, the second wife started treating them cruelly and starving them to death.

The two children regularly visited their mother's grave and sat there crying. One day a candy stick grew there, and they started sucking at it whenever they felt hungry. After that they began to grow healthy and strong. Their stepmother noticed the change and asked them what they were feeding on. They told her frogs. So the next day she asked them to take her daughter with them to eat some frogs. They did as she asked and showed her daughter a frog in the river. When the daughter tried to catch it, it jumped on her and pricked her eyes. Her mother was terrified to see her only daughter completely blind. The other two children explained to her that her daughter simply did not know how to catch frogs.

A few days later, the woman was keeping a close watch on them and eventually discovered their secret source of food. Out of sheer revenge she uprooted the candy stick, opened up the grave, and scattered the bones of their mother.

One day the father was going away on a journey. He asked his children what they wanted him to buy them. The others asked for nice clothes and toys, but Nunja, the daughter of his late wife, asked for a pomegranate instead. When he returned, he brought his children what they had asked for.

At this same time the sultan invited people to gather in his palace to attend a "spinning wool party." The whole family went except for Nunja, because her stepmother had contrived to keep her busy. She had scattered a large amount of grain and told Nunja to pick it up. A crow came flying by and noticed what she was doing. He landed in front of her, and she asked him to help her.

"I'll do it as quickly as possible," he said, "if you'll promise to give me a piece of cloth to furnish my nest."

She promptly agreed. In no time the crow had picked up all the grain. Nunja was now able to go to the party. She went into the house and tried to find some nice clothes to wear. Unfortunately, all she had were old tatters. She looked around and, quite by chance, came across the pomegranate. She opened it up and was surprised to find inside the very finest clothes and a fantastic pair of shoes. She put them on and rushed to the sultan's palace. During the entire party her stepmother failed to recognize her.

Just before the party's festivities were over, Nunja left unnoticed. In a rush to leave the palace, she lost one of her shoes. She was so scared of her stepmother that she could not go back to look for her shoe.

A slave happened to pass by and came across the gleaming shoe. He had never seen anything like it before. He immediately took it to his master and gave it to him. The sultan was amazed and ordered that all females should return to his palace. They were all questioned, but no woman or girl had ever seen such a shoe.

Next day every house was searched, and eventually it emerged that Nunja was the owner of the shoe. The sultan asked her father for her hand, and he readily accepted.

During the wedding ceremony, the stepmother sat with Nunja, with her own blind daughter, Aakasha, beside her. The stepmother kept weeping, pretending that she was going to miss Nunja very much. She kept patting her on the head and shoulders and managed secretly to insert a needle in her head. Nunja immediately turned into a white dove and flew out of the palace. The stepmother then dressed up her own daughter as a bride. When the sultan was led into his bride's chamber, he noticed the difference in her features but said nothing. Thus, Aakasha became his wife and bore him a son. The dove returned to the palace garden and nested on top of reeds.

When harvest season came, workers began to cut down the reeds. The dove started to sing: "Beneath the joints, upon the joints of the reeds, be careful not to cut hennaed fingers!"

The dove kept leaping from one reed to another and thus managed to distract the workers so they would not cut the reeds down. The sultan came out and found them all sitting idly. He was angry and ordered them to get on with their task. So they cut down all the reeds. When they reached the very last one, the dove jumped into the sultan's lap. He was amused and held the dove in his hands. He took the bird inside and gave it to his wife, Aakasha. "Look at this beautiful dove!" he said. "Take care of it."

Later, when Aakasha suspected the dove of being a mysterious creature, she asked her husband to kill it. He refused and insisted on protecting it. Whenever the sultan went away on business, Aakasha plucked a feather from the dove and blamed it on her child.

One day the sultan took the dove and sat in the garden, caressing it affectionately. Suddenly, his fingers came upon a needle planted in its head. He pulled it out, and immediately the dove became Nunja herself in flesh and blood. He recognized her on the spot.

He took her into a private room and asked her what had happened. She told him the whole story. The sultan then slaughtered Aakasha, cut her into pieces, and sent them to her mother as a present. The mother was delighted that her daughter was sending her meat. To let her neighbors know the good news, she sent them some of the meat. But when she came to wash the rest of the meat for cooking, she came upon her own daughter's nose. She was stunned and fell down dead.

The Ghoul and the Cow
[17]

ONCE UPON A TIME there was a man who lived close to a forest. He raised cattle and wished he had a son to help him when he grew up. His wife became pregnant and fulfilled his wish, he being the only child they had. The father was very happy and doted on his son. In fact, he loved him more than all the land and the cattle he owned.

When the son grew up, his father started sending him to the forest to watch the cows. One day a cow slipped on a rock and broke its leg. By the time the son collected the cattle to take them back home, night had already fallen. Even so, he could not simply leave the disabled cow there because the wolves would devour it before morning. So he went to his father and told him what had happened. They decided that the cow had to be saved at all costs. The father brought a knife, slaughtered the cow, and removed the hide. The meat had to be carried home and sold the next day. Father and son were both already starving and tired, and to carry all that meat home would require a lot of energy. The father had an idea: they would roast the liver and eat it first. "Go and look for some fire," he told his son.

The son walked about in the forest and spotted a fire not too far away. He thought it might belong to a bushman or journeyman. He went over there and found a ghoul sitting by the fire warming himself. At the sight of the ghoul, the child was horrified. He tried to sneak away, but it was too late. The ghoul had become aware of his presence. "What do you want, boy?" he said.

"Some fire, please."

"All right. Come over here and take me on your back."

The son had no choice and went back to his father with the ghoul on his back. When his father saw him, he said, "Oh, my son, you brought someone who's going to eat us tonight."

When the son bent down to let the ghoul down, his leg twisted under the weight and broke.

"I'm going to eat you and your son," the ghoul told the father.

"You are welcome," the father replied. "It's our fate. Please start with the cow; it's all ready. Look at this wonderful, fresh red meat."

While the ghoul was busy devouring the cow, the father put his son on his back and slipped away into the forest, leaving the entire herd of cows behind.

When they had emerged from the forest and were safely at home, the son said, "But father, you left all the cows!"

"Come, my son," he replied without the slightest hint of regret, "you're my real capital. Cows can be replaced, but you can't."

The Ostrich Hunter

[18]

FOR A LONG TIME a man was trying to catch ostriches, but he always failed. When he bought a gun, he became more self-confident. However, he still went out hunting every day, only to return empty-handed. In fact, the ostriches proved particularly difficult since they could smell a man many miles away and run away as fast as lightning.

One day he woke up from a dream still laughing.

"Why are you laughing?" his wife inquired.

"Oh, now I've got it!" he said. "It's taken me years of thinking and planning to catch an ostrich, and it was all a waste of time. In a single dream you can get the best of ideas! Last night I dreamed the solution."

So he went to the market and bought a large number of ostrich feathers. It took him a few days more to sew them on a garment. When he put it on, he looked exactly like an ostrich. Next morning he went out into the desert, strutting along like an ostrich and hiding the gun inside his garment.

When he reached the spot where the ostriches were feeding, he got his gun ready. He kept moving ahead surely and slowly. All of a sudden a gunshot exploded not far from where he was. He felt his heart warm and then fell unconscious.

Another hunter was close by. When he had spotted him, he had assumed it was an ostrich. Taking aim he had shot him dead. When the other hunter realized what he had done, he exclaimed, "Sooner or later the ostrich hunter will get his deserts!"

Jackal and Hedgehog

[19]

ONCE UPON A TIME a jackal and a hedgehog were good friends. One day they agreed to steal beans from a peasant's underground stock. They discussed their plan of action. The hedgehog volunteered to go down into the *thasraft* to fill the sacks with beans. When the jackal pulled up the last sack, he said, "Good-bye, my friend."

The hedgehog felt betrayed. "How can you leave me in this trap?" he asked.

"Right now it's not so bad," the jackal replied. "But just wait until tomorrow morning when the peasant arrives and finds you!"

The hedgehog had to think fast to find a way out. "All right, my friend," he told the jackal in a pitiful tone. "Please take one sack along to my children."

The hedgehog filled up the sack, then dived into it himself, hiding under the beans. The jackal pulled the heavy sack out and then left.

On the road, the hedgehog put out his head and started whistling. The jackal thought it was the peasant approaching and ran away fast. When he reached the hedgehog's children, he told them the peasant had caught their father. But before he had even finished his sentence, the hedgehog jumped out laughing. "Thank God," said the hedgehog, "now I know you for what you are!"

Sometime later, they agreed to go hunting together. They came across a herd of sheep. The hedgehog was assigned to keep the shepherd busy while the jackal snatched a sheep and ran away with it. When the hedgehog was sure the jackal had escaped, he followed him.

When they reached a valley, they slaughtered the sheep and took off the skin. Suddenly, the hedgehog shouted, "The shepherd is coming!"

Frightened, the jackal ran away and disappeared from sight. The hedgehog took the entire sheep and went home with it.

Later, the hedgehog was making a meal for his children. The jackal smelled it cooking and asked him for a bowl. When he had tasted it, he said, "Oh, how delicious it is! It tastes rich. Where did you get the fat?"

"I pulled it from my armpits," replied the hedgehog. To convince the jackal, he had hidden a piece of sheep's fat under his armpit and used it to give him a demonstration.

The jackal went away and tried the trick again and again. Every day he tried taking fat from his armpits until it became very painful. Then he started to bleed and died.

Wolf and Hedgehog

[20]

I

A WOLF AND A HEDGEHOG were always trying to outwit each other. One day the wolf challenged the hedgehog: "I have one hundred and one stratagems."

To which the hedgehog humbly replied, "I've got just one and a half."

When winter came and they had scarcely any food left for their children, they decided to steal barley from the *metmoura* of a neighbor. After midnight, they took a sack, a rope, and a bucket and set off. When they got there, they argued over who would go down to fill the bucket. The wolf outwitted the hedgehog, arguing that he was heavier and too large for the bucket. "Listen," he said, "you're smaller and can roll like a ball. It'll be easier to pull you up in the bucket."

The hedgehog was convinced and accepted the decision. He rolled himself up like a thorny ball and lay in the bottom of the bucket. The wolf tied the rope to the bucket and let him down. The hedgehog started filling the bucket and sending it up. The wolf filled the sack. The last bucketful had been emptied into the sack. "Farewell, my friend!" said the wolf to the hedgehog. "And thank you very much."

"What do you mean?" the hedgehog whispered. "Send me down the bucket and get me out of this hole."

"I don't care—good-bye!"

"How dare you leave me in this trap?"

The hedgehog started pleading with the wolf, but the wolf just laughed at him. Finally, the hedgehog admitted his defeat. "All right," he admitted. "You've won. But please send the bucket down so I can fill it for my children."

The wolf let the bucket down. The hedgehog filled it up. Before jumping in and covering himself with barley, he shouted, "Pull!" The wolf pulled the bucket up, emptied it in his sack, and departed. All along the road the wolf was imagining the scene when the owner of barley would arrive and find the hedgehog. That made him laugh at the sheer stupidity of the hedgehog. "It pays to be clever!" he told himself.

When the wolf got home, the hedgehog's children were the first to meet him. When they did not see their father, they started crying. "Don't cry!" said the wolf. "I'll give you some of my food. I'm so sorry your father is—."

Suddenly, the hedgehog jumped out of the sack onto the wolf's shoulder. "Thank you so much, my friend," he said, "for carrying me on your shoulders all the way here!"

II

Days passed, and yet again the wolf came to the hedgehog and invited him out on another night expedition. It was summer, and a farm nearby was full of ripe vegetables and juicy fruits.

Around the farm was a thick hedge of thorny plants. To get in, each of them had to dig a hole his own size. Once inside they started eating. Every so often the hedgehog reminded the wolf: "Eat by all means, Uncle Wolf, but don't forget your size."

The wolf was really hungry and greedy, so he did not even try to understand what the hedgehog's words meant. Whenever the hedgehog finished eating a fruit, he went back to his hole in the hedge to make sure he could still get through. By now the hole was only just wide enough.

"Uncle Wolf," he said, "it's almost dawn. We have to go home. The farmer and his sons will be here soon."

So each went back to his hole. The hedgehog slipped out easily, but the wolf was too big and could hardly squeeze through. He was stuck. Light was already spreading from the east. Now he begged the hedgehog to give him an idea.

"All right," the hedgehog said. "I've already used one trick. I've only got a half left."

"Please, lend me that half to get out of this trap."

"But what happened to your hundred and one?" the hedgehog asked.

"Oh, I'm so full, I can't think of anything. Please, help me."

"Now, listen, my friend," said the hedgehog. "Go back to the middle of the farm. Lie down on your back. Open your mouth and let flies get in and out freely. Don't move. When the farmer and his sons arrive, they'll think you're dead. They'll immediately throw you out before you start rotting and spoil their fruits and vegetables. This is the best plan for your escape."

The wolf appreciated the plan and thanked the hedgehog.

That morning the farmer and his sons arrived and discovered the wolf still lying there motionlessly. Seeing him in that state, they started laughing. "Just look at our enemy! It serves him right. He's eaten more than his stomach can hold. Quick, boys, he'll be going rotten soon and fill the whole place with stench. Ugh! Pull him out."

As soon as they had thrown the wolf over the hedge, he sprang to his feet and sped away like an arrow, raising a cloud of dust behind him. The farmer and his sons just stood there, stunned by the trick the wolf had played on them and rubbing their hands together in frustration and anger.

III

The donkey had seen what had happened and started laughing aloud. The farmer felt humiliated and kicked the donkey on his backside, but the donkey kept laughing.

"Why are you laughing, you stupid beast?" the farmer asked.

"Because you were fooled by a mere wolf!"

"And do you think you're more clever?"

"I cannot say that, sir, but I can defeat him."

"Tell me, what's your idea?"

"I promise I can catch him for you."

"All right, what's the deal?"

"A whole sack of barley and a month's holiday."

"You'll have your wish, but if you don't catch him, I'll make you work harder and no food."

"Agreed!"

That night the donkey went to the hole where the wolf lived with his family. He stretched on his back right in front of the mouth of the hole and lay dead still. He opened his mouth and let flies in and out.

Early next morning the she-wolf woke up and was the first to go out for fresh air. She discovered the donkey motionless, with legs in the air and flies going in and out of his mouth and backside. She smiled and went back inside. She waited until her husband woke up, pretending she had not been out yet. When the wolf opened his eyes, she yawned. "Oh, what a dream I had last night!" she said.

"I hope it's a good one."

"I dreamed of big game right at the mouth of our hole. Enough food for a month."

"I hope your dream will come true."

The wolf walked out and was surprised to find a huge donkey, swollen, eyes open, and flies going in and out. He returned to his wife and kissed her. "Oh, Zermana, my great dreamer," he said. "Come, come, there's a donkey outside."

Pretending to be surprised that her dream had been realized, she walked out with him to see for herself.

They started thinking of how to get the donkey inside. None of their plans seemed likely to work. Suddenly, the wolf remembered his neighbor, the hedgehog, the one with bright ideas. He went to see him and asked for help. The hedgehog came and examined the donkey carefully. He could sense that the donkey was still alive, but kept quiet about it. "It's easy," he told the wolf. "Bring a rope. Your wife will tie it tightly to your tail, and then you'll pull him while she pushes from the head."

The wolf did what he was told. When his tail was firmly attached to the donkey's tail, the hedgehog shouted, "Now, pull!"

Suddenly, the donkey sprang to his feet and ran off as fast as a hare, dragging the wolf behind him. The hedgehog rolled on the ground, laughing away. The wolf's wife tried to come to her husband's aid, but she could not do anything. "Grab hold of plants and trees!" she yelled to him.

But the donkey was too fast and too powerful for the wolf to do anything. "Oh, Zermana," he shouted back at his wife, "you're a lousy dreamer! I'm gone, gone!"

All that could be seen now was a cloud of dust. The donkey was galloping as fast as a rocket. In no time he reached the farm and delivered the wolf to the farmer and his sons. Thereafter, the donkey was rewarded with what he had been promised, and the wolf was severely punished.

The Hunter and the Two Partridges

[21]

LONG BEFORE he got married, a man enjoyed living among family and friends. When he met a woman and agreed to live together like husband and wife, she made it clear that she wanted a home of her own. He welcomed the suggestion and built a house in the village where he could see his relatives and friends every day. But the woman kept complaining about a lack of intimacy; she wanted to retire to a place farther away, near the forest. At first he resisted, but her constant bad mood forced him to move to an abode on the edge of the forest.

There the woman was always happy, but the man felt lonely. Although the distance between forest and village was close, he felt abandoned by his family and friends. In fact, he now realized that even when he was still in the village, they had already started ignoring him. He felt miserable and spent most of the time thinking why their attitude toward him had changed.

One day he went into the forest and caught two fat partridges. He felt happy and brought them back home to his wife. On his way he met an old friend and felt the urge to invite him to lunch. When the wife saw the partridges, she was very delighted and praised her husband as the best of hunters. He then told her that they had a guest that day. On hearing that, his wife did not seem very pleased, but she did not show it. Her husband went back to the forest. He sat talking and laughing with his friend while they waited for lunchtime.

In the kitchen the wife plucked the birds and started cooking them. The delicious smell went to her head, and her mouth started watering. When she was turning them over in the pot, she cut a piece of meat to see if it was well cooked. With each piece her appetite increased, and she kept eating until she had finished the first partridge. Then she ate the second and drank the sauce. When she had her fill, she lay down and thought what she could do to save her husband from embarrassment. After some time she reached a satisfactory conclusion. Her plan was ready for execution.

Soon it was lunchtime, and her husband and his guest arrived. They sat in the guest room, drinking tea and waiting for lunch to be served. An hour or so after tea, they started feeling really hungry. The husband started looking gloomy and wondering why his wife was taking so long. He sprang nervously to his feet and went into the kitchen. There he found his wife dozing. "Haven't you finished cooking yet?" he yelled.

"Well," she replied, "I've been waiting for you to come and whet this knife to cut the bread."

He snatched the knife and went out to a rock near the house. Meanwhile, she slipped into the guest room. "For God's sake," she whispered to the guest, "save yourself from death!"

"What's the matter?"

"Look over there. My husband's sharpening the knife to cut your ear."

The guest looked out and saw his host bending over the rock. The blade was flashing in the sun. He realized the danger he was in, so he sneaked out and started running away as fast as he could, raising the dust behind him. Now the wife shouted to her husband, "Your guest has made off with the two partridges! Go and catch him!"

Still holding the knife, the husband chased after him. "Stop!

Stop!" he yelled at the top of his voice. "Give me just one and keep the other for yourself."

The guest was still running but turned around in fright. "If you catch me," he said, "I'll give you both."

With all speed the guest disappeared into the forest like a hare. Feeling hungry and betrayed, the husband ran for a few more meters, then collapsed on the ground. His wife helped him back home.

Thereafter, the old friend spread the rumor that the man had a fetish about ears and would invite people for a meal but only in order to cut off their ears. People now began to suspect that was why he had moved out of the village in order to live near the forest. The rumor soon spread throughout the entire neighborhood, and they left the man and his wife alone forever.

Three Sisters

[22]

WHEN A MAN'S WIFE DIED, he was left with three young daughters. Unable to raise them by himself, he married another woman so she could help him. However, when she realized how much he loved them, she started thinking of ways to get rid of them. Every day when they sat down to eat, she used to serve him just sauce, but no meat. When he complained, she blamed it all on his daughters. "If it's meat you want," she told him, "then get rid of those girls."

One day he took the three daughters to a forest and abandoned them there. When night came and their father did not return, they started looking for a shelter. They saw a light glimmering and walked toward it. A mother ghoul opened the door and invited them in. They told her their story, and she took pity on them. She warned them that she had three savage, dangerous sons who ate human beings. But since they had nowhere else to go, she promised to hide them when her sons were in the house.

When her sons arrived, they smelled something different in the house. They asked their mother if there was anyone there, but she covered up the fact that the three girls were there. The brothers did not believe their mother and started whispering among themselves. They decided to leave one of them at home the next day to keep a watch on things.

Next day, when the mother ghoul woke up, she found one of her sons still in the house. She asked him why he had not gone out with his brothers. He pretended to be sick and tired, so she put a sleeping powder in his drink and he fell asleep for the entire day. She then let the sisters out of their hiding place and fed them.

When night fell and the other brothers returned home, they questioned their brother, but he told them he had not seen anyone. They guessed what their mother had done. Next day the youngest brother stayed behind, and his mother tried to give him the same powder, but he poured it into his lap. He lay down and pretended he had fallen asleep. The mother called out the three sisters and gave them some food. He snatched a quick look at them and was fascinated by their beauty. All of a sudden he leaped out of bed and told them not to be afraid.

When his brothers came back home, they found him sitting and laughing with the three beautiful girls.

They all reassured the girls that they were quite safe. The mother ghoul was stunned to see her children behaving so gently and kindly to the sisters. Next day they were all happily married.

Years went by, and the sisters' father regretted what he had done. He came to hate his wife for playing the trick on him that deprived him of his own children. First he killed her, then set off in quest of his daughters. When he grew tired of his travels, the only house he found close by was the house of the ghouls who had married his daughters. He asked them for hospitality, and they made him welcome. When he saw his daughters, he recognized them and claimed them as his own children. However, they denied him and urged their husbands to get rid of this stranger.

Next day he returned home, depressed and dejected. He remained alone in the house for a long time with no food or water until eventually he died.

Aisha and the Black Cat

[23]

A MAN WAS MARRIED to two wives, each of whom gave him a daughter. Tabla was the name of the daughter of the first wife, and Aisha of the second. Tabla was ugly and very spoiled by her mother, while Aisha was beautiful and hardworking. When Aisha's mother died, the first wife treated her like a servant. However, the father loved and admired Aisha more and started defending her against his second wife. The latter started getting jealous and decided to take her revenge on Aisha.

One day when the father was away, she threw her out of the house. "If you stay here," she said, "I'll poison you. You can come back only if you bring me a bag of gold and silver."

The woman knew it was impossible for the young girl to find such a treasure. Aisha was very upset and went off weeping. Leaving the house behind her, she walked farther and farther until darkness fell and she found herself in a forest.

It was very cold and rainy. She crouched for shelter under a tree, but soon she heard wild animals howling and roaring. She was very frightened and kept peering through the impenetrable darkness. Suddenly, she saw a light flickering somewhere and walked toward it. Eventually, she reached an old house. At the door she encountered a black cat that started mewing and coiling itself around her legs. She called out, but no one answered. She stroked the cat, then picked it up in her arms and kissed it. She went inside and found a cozy corner. There she slept the whole night with the cat in her embrace.

When she woke up next morning, she found no cat, as though it had all been just a dream. Then she heard a child talking to his mother in the next room. He was telling her how a young woman had saved him from the cold and rain and had taken care of him the whole night. Aisha suddenly thought this might be a jinn's house, so she tried getting away through a door. Suddenly, she felt herself restrained by a set of long claws that clasped her by the shoulder. Shutting her eyes, she prayed for safe deliverance. However, what she heard was a motherly voice cooing in her ears: "You've nothing to fear, daughter." When she opened her eyes and looked around, she saw an old mother ghoul holding a child. He smiled up at her.

"This is the woman," he told his mother, "the one who was very kind to me and saved me from the rain and cold."

The mother ghoul thanked her for taking care of her child, but Aisha did not recognize him. Being totally honest as she was, she said, "Frankly, I've never seen this child before. In fact, what I found was a black cat. Where is it?"

The mother laughed. "You are absolutely right," she said. "Whenever I go out, I turn my child into a cat for his own protection. When I come home again, I turn him back into a child."

Aisha had heard such stories and was not unduly surprised. The mother ghoul then asked her why she had come to the forest. Aisha told her the whole story of her stepmother and how miserable she had been since her mother's death. The mother ghoul took pity on her and invited her to stay as long she liked, but Aisha expressed her desire to return home because she loved her father so much.

Grateful to her for taking care of her child, the ghoula then gave her a bag full of gold and silver. Aisha kissed both mother and child good-bye and departed very happy.

Thus, she returned home carrying the treasure. When her step-mother saw what she had brought in the bag, she kissed her and welcomed her home.

She summoned her daughter, Tabla. "Just look at what Aisha has brought me!" she said. "Now you go away and bring me the same thing, or else you're not my daughter."

Tabla was crushed to see her mother favoring Aisha and turning against her. She went away very unhappy and followed the very same road.

At night she saw a light and searched for it. In front of an old house she was met by a black cat that kept mewing and coiling itself around her legs. She lost her temper and kicked it away. Entering the house, she shut the door behind her and left the cat crying in the cold and rain.

Next morning Tabla woke up and heard a child telling his mother about a nasty woman who had treated him badly the previous night. The mother ghoul became very angry. She thrust her claws into Tabla's neck and devoured her.

The Spinster Frog

[24]

A FEMALE FROG was getting old. No one had ever asked to marry her or bothered even to look at her. Every day she showed herself in front of her house, but in vain. One day a man saw her looking miserable. "What's your problem?" he asked.

"I'm looking for a husband," she replied, "but I'm struck with bad luck. No one even bothers to look at me."

"It's not a question of luck. Listen to me. Make yourself attractive. Put something red on your cheeks and wear some nice clothes."

She did her best to alter her appearance and then stood in front of her door, waiting. A donkey passed by, looked at her, and liked her. "Oh, beautiful frog," he asked, "will you marry me?"

"Yes, I will," she said, "but first sing to me."

The donkey brayed at the top of his voice. She put her hands over her ears. "You've scared me," she yelled at him. "Go away."

When the donkey went away disappointed, she regretted her reaction and was just about to call him back when a mouse appeared. He stood looking up at her with admiration. "How lovely you are!" he whispered timidly. "I'm looking for a wife. Will you accept me?"

"First let me hear you sing," she said.

The mouse made some very high squeaks, but even so she welcomed him. Next day the mouse brought her bracelets and anklets of gold, and they got married. She asked him what his job was. He told her he was working at the king's palace. She was impressed and thanked God for her luck.

One day she went down to the river to wash her husband's clothes. She slipped and fell in the river. As she started shouting for help, the king himself happened to be riding nearby and heard her. When she saw him, she said, "Please send my husband the mouse to come and rescue me."

The king was amazed that a frog could not swim but could talk like a human being. He laughed and went away to tell his wife about this strange and amusing story.

Back in the palace the king was entertaining his wife by telling her what he had heard. The mouse, who happened to be in the king's bedroom trying to steal more jewelry, rushed out through a hole in the wall and went straight to the river.

There he found his wife still struggling to keep her head above water. When he tried to pull her by her hands, she was afraid of losing her bracelets. Then he tried to drag her out by the feet, but again she shouted at him that she might lose her anklets. Finally, he grabbed her by the waist, but the bracelets and the anklets were so heavy that they both drowned.

The Girl in the River

[25]

A MAN HAD a daughter and a son. When their mother died, he married another woman to have her take care of them, but she hated them and urged her husband to get rid of them. He took the children to a forest. However, his daughter guessed what his plan was and concealed some bran under her clothes that she dropped all the way there. The father left them in the forest, pretending that he would come back. Meanwhile, they were able to trace their way back home by following the trail of bran. That night the girl hid in the mule trough, and her brother used the cow trough.

Next morning when the wife and her husband arrived to feed the animals, they found the children there. The woman scolded her husband for not obeying her. This time he took them to the cavern of ghouls and left them to their fate. At night the female ghoul was the first to return to the cavern and discovered the children, who looked gaunt and famished. She told them her husband would eat them as soon as he set eyes on them, so she had to hide them from him. She took them to a stock of dates. They were very happy that the female ghoul was being so nice to them, but actually what she had in mind was simply to fatten them up and keep them all for herself.

After a while the sister and brother got fat and strong. The male ghoul discovered them and was getting ready to eat them. They were very frightened and quickly dug a deep hole under the door. When he charged at them, he fell into it. Then they burned him.

Finally, the female ghoul came over to them. Once she saw how fat they had become, her mouth started watering. She talked to them in a motherly tone and asked them to help her build a fire. They gathered a lot of wood and started the fire. They all waited for it to catch, but it was too slow. The ghoul was getting impatient and asked them to get closer and blow on it. But they claimed not to have any breath and suggested that she do it herself. As she got closer to the fire, they pushed her in and watched her burn.

Thereafter, brother and sister lived in peace and security. Time passed, and they both grew up. Every day the brother went into the forest to watch the cattle, while the sister would climb to the top of a tree and keep an eye on him. Just below the tree there flowed a wide river.

One day a horseman stopped by to let his horse drink. Suddenly, in the river he saw the reflection of a beautiful woman. He thought it must be a mermaid and went straight to the king to inform him.

The king sent his soldiers to catch her. When they reached the river, the girl was very thirsty and was about to climb down to take a drink. However, she was reluctant to take her eyes off her brother, so she asked the men to give her some water. Looking up, they saw a beautiful young girl with very long hair. They asked her to let her hair drop so they could use it as a rope. Once she had done that, they pulled her down and took her to the king. As soon as he saw her, he fell in love and asked her to marry him. She accepted on condition that her brother could live in the palace with them. When her brother was sent for and told the news, he was very delighted. He left the forest to live in the palace. From then on they all lived happily together.

M'Hirez the Adopted Child

[26]

AN OLD COUPLE was childless. They had just one servant living with them. They found an orphan child to adopt and named him M'Hirez.

One day the old man brought some meat home and asked his wife to cook it. But the old woman was greedy; she ate it all herself and blamed it on the child.

The old man gave M'Hirez a severe beating. The child felt he had been unjustly punished. He went outside and sat by the wall crying.

"Why are you crying?" the wall asked.

"Because the old woman ate the meat," he replied, "but the old man beat me."

"I'm going to collapse," said the wall in sympathy.

Pigeons arrived and found the wall crumbled. "Why did you collapse?" they asked.

"Because the old woman ate the meat, and yet the old man beat the child."

"And we shall pluck our feathers," said the pigeons.

The tree saw the pigeons completely featherless. "Why did you pluck your feathers?" it asked.

"Because the old woman ate the meat, but the old man beat the child. And the wall collapsed."

"And I shall shed all my leaves."

The cow came along looking for some shade. "Why did you shed your leaves?" she asked.

"Because the old woman ate the meat, but the old man beat the child. Then the wall collapsed, and the pigeons plucked their feathers."

"And I shall break my horns."

The cow went down to the river for a drink. "Why did you break your horns?" the river asked.

"Because the old woman ate the meat, the old man beat the child, the wall collapsed, the pigeons plucked their feathers, and the tree shed its leaves."

"And I shall dry up my water."

The servant came down to the river to fill her jar but found it dry. "Why did you dry up your water?" she asked.

"Because the old woman ate the meat, the old man beat the child, the wall collapsed, the pigeons plucked their feathers, the tree shed its leaves, and the cow broke its horns."

"And I shall break the jar."

The old woman saw the servant coming back without the jar. "What happened to the jar?" she asked.

The servant explained to her why. "In that case," the woman said, "I shall kill myself."

The Girl and the Fakih

[27]

A WIDOWER LIVED with his two daughters just opposite a mosque. The older daughter did the housework, and the younger one tended to a small bed of mint in front of the door. Whenever she was out, she sensed the *fakih*'s eyes staring at her from the top of the mosque minaret. He was always trying to attract her attention, and it embarrassed her. He was as old as her father, was married, and had children of his own. What shocked and disgusted her above all about his behavior was that he was venerated as a holy man.

After many vain attempts he decided to pose her a question. "How many leaves are there in your patch of mint?" he asked.

She had enough imagination to understand his insinuation and was disgusted. "As many as the words in your book," she replied. "Why don't you count them to keep yourself busy? Then you'll stop bothering me!"

Her sarcastic response infuriated him, and he vowed to take his revenge. His earlier infatuation was now completely turned into hatred.

Days went by, and he sent a few people to act on his behalf in asking her father for her hand. The father did not object and was even honored that such a holy man would be his son-in-law. Without even consulting his daughter, he accepted. The following day a wedding ceremony took place.

During that day the bride was in the company of her aunt, who advised her on marriage matters. The girl opened her heart to her aunt. When the aunt understood the story, she provided her niece with a bag of wax to take along with her hidden among her personal belongings.

So it happened that when night fell and the bride was admitted to the *fakih*'s private room, she asked the women to leave her alone for a while so she could change her clothes. She stuffed her clothes with wax and laid them on the bed, then dressed herself in old rags and left the room disguised as a beggar. Just before midnight, she stole out of the house and disappeared into the dark night.

Meanwhile, the groom was led into his room. People waited outside, expecting him to show them a sign of virginity. Once inside he took a knife and stabbed the bride in bed. His revenge was going to be to drink her blood. He pulled the knife out to taste her blood and realized it was sweet. Suspecting something, he took off her clothes and discovered only wax. When he realized that she had managed to outwit him and subvert his cunning plan, his desire for revenge intensified. His sense of manliness was affronted, and he suffered a heart attack.

As dawn broke, the witnesses ran out of patience. Entering the room to see what was happening, they discovered to their horror that the *fakih* was dead cold and the bride was not to be found. They searched the bed and found that she had been turned into a wax doll. When the news was reported, people were not surprised because such phenomena were very common among them. They blamed the whole tragedy on some witch who must have been jealous of the *fakih* and his new bride. Some people suspected his first wife, and they immediately started searching for her. But she was nowhere to be found.

The Modest Girl

[28]

A MAN WAS MARRIED and had only one daughter. Her mother died, so her father married again. His new wife also gave him a daughter.

The two half sisters did not get on well with each other, so the second wife started making life difficult for the stepdaughter. When she sent them down to the river to bring water, she gave her own daughter a bucket and the stepdaughter a sieve. As a result the latter was beaten every single day for not bringing any water.

One day the stepdaughter kept trying to fill the sieve, but it slipped from her grasp and was carried away by the river. When she returned home without it, she was severely punished, then told to go back and look for it.

The poor girl followed the course of the river, looking for the sieve. When she came across a gardener, she asked him if he had seen a sieve. He told her first to help him remove the weeds from his garden. When she had finished, he showed her a few women washing wool by the river. "Go and ask them," he said. "They know."

Again, the women asked her to help them first, which she did.

When she had finished, they pointed out an old house. "The woman who lives there knows," they said.

When she knocked on the door, it was already dark. A strange old woman opened the door. "Do you want to come in through the door," she asked, "or through a hole?"

"Just as you wish," the girl replied.

The woman let her in through the door. "Now," she asked, "do you want me to slay a sheep or a dog for your dinner?"

"Anything you like."

The woman slew a sheep and cooked it. "Do you want bread made of flour or ash?" she asked.

"As you wish," she replied once more.

The woman made flour bread, and they had a good dinner. Afterward, the woman asked the girl if she wanted henna or cow's dung on her hands. The girl answered in the same way as before. Then they went to sleep.

Next morning when the girl woke up, she found a horse standing in front of the door carrying two bags full of gold. Eager to take leave of her hostess and to thank her for her hospitality, she called out to her. The woman answered from another room where she had concealed herself. "Take that horse with you," she said. "You can't see me in daylight."

The girl did what she was told and left.

When she arrived home, the girl left the horse with the treasure outside and went in. When her stepmother saw she had come back without the sieve, she dismissed her with some harsh words. The girl went out to look for her father. She showed him what she had brought, and they both went to live in a separate house. While the father was opening the bags and weighing the gold, his wife was spying on him through a hole in the wall. She heard what his daughter told him and went back home.

The following day she gave her own daughter another sieve. She told her to throw it in the river and follow it just as her half sister had done. At first her daughter refused, but her mother threatened to throw her out of the house; with that she reluctantly left to follow in her half sister's steps. She came upon the same people. The gardener asked her to help him, but she refused. When the women asked her to help them, she said she was not born a servant. Finally, she reached the old woman's house at nightfall.

"Do you want to come in through the door or a hole?" she asked.

"I'm not a rat," she replied. "I'll come through the door."

The woman let her in. "Now" she asked, "do you want me to slay a sheep or a dog for your dinner?"

"I'm not a hyena. I want sheep."

"And do you want bread made of flour or ash?"

"Ash? Are you mad?"

The woman gave her food and then let her go to sleep.

In the morning she found a horse standing there with two bags. She leaped on it and rode away without saying good-bye to the woman, thinking she was still asleep.

So she returned to her mother very happy. They both kept quiet about the treasure and waited until nighttime, then opened the bags to weigh the treasure. But the two bags were full of snakes and scorpions. They sprang at mother and daughter and killed them on the spot.

The Mother Goat

[29]

THE MOTHER GOAT lived alone with her young kids. When she decided to go out to bring them water and food, she warned them not to open the door for anyone. A wolf was spying on her. When she left, he came to the door.

"Open up," he said. "I've food and water for you."

The kids recognized his voice. "Go away," they said, "or our mother will come and kill you with her horns."

The wolf waited for a while. Then he came back and imitated her voice. The kids were happy and opened the door. He sprang on them and carried them back to his lair.

Shortly afterward, the mother goat returned but did not find her children. She guessed it could only be the wolf and ran to his home. She jumped on his roof and started trampling with her feet.

"Stop it, stop it!" the wolf yelled. "You're destroying the home I built with my claws and teeth."

But the she-goat kept jumping up and down, forcing her hooves into the roof. When dust started falling on the wolf's head, he went outside to chase her. She charged at him with her sharp horns and tore him to pieces. Thus, she managed to retrieve her kids unharmed and went back home very happy.

A Donkey Named Fritla

[30]

A MAN OWNED a young donkey that he named Fritla because, no matter what he did, the donkey always managed to slip away from him. One day the donkey escaped and disappeared. The man went out and looked everywhere. He encountered a group of hunters. "Have you seen a donkey," he asked, "one that always slips away, named Fritla?"

The hunters were very angry, pounced on him, and gave him a good beating. When he had had enough, he asked them, "Why are you beating me?"

"Because that name's a bad omen. Now we won't catch any game today. It's already slipped away from us."

"So, tell me, please, what should I say?"

"You must say: 'I hope that every day you'll bring fifty.'"

He left them, saying the sentence over and over to himself. Then he met some mourners carrying a dead woman to a graveyard. He stopped them and said, "I hope you'll bring fifty every day."

Putting down the corpse, they too started beating him severely.

"Please stop!" he yelled. "What should I say?"

"You should say: 'May God have mercy on her soul and commiserate with her relatives.'"

He went away, again turning the sentence over in his mind. Next he saw a crowd of people bringing a bride to the house of the groom. He stopped them. "May God have mercy on her soul," he said, "and commiserate with her relatives."

They were very angry and gave him a good beating.

"Please," he asked them, "tell me, what's the right thing to say?"

"You should say: 'May God make her feel at home, provide her with the wherewithal to live, and never leave the place.'"

So he continued on his way until he found a few peasants fighting locusts.

"May God make her feel at home," he said, "provide her with the wherewithal to live, and never leave the place."

Infuriated, they gathered around him with their sticks and beat him. He begged them to stop. "What should I say instead?" he asked.

"May it retreat farther to where you can never see it."

He resumed his search until he came across some people collecting salt from the edge of a lake.

"May it retreat farther to where you can never see it," he said.

They hit him with their shovels until he cried for mercy. "Please tell me," he asked. "What should I say?"

"May the next be dry just as soon as you finish the first one."

Later he found farmers irrigating fig trees.

"May the next be dry," he said, "just as soon as you finish the first one."

They beat him, too, telling him, "What you should say is: 'May they become ripe and fall.'"

Next he came across some people building a mosque. He repeated the previous sentence and was beaten again. They told him, "Say: 'May you pray in it and your children's children.'"

He met a few people digging a well. "May you pray in it," he said, "and your children's children."

He was beaten and advised to say, "May you dig down one meter and find water."

Then he came upon people digging a hole to store barley in it. "May you dig down one meter," he said, "and find water."

He was punished, but by now he could take no more beating.

"I don't want him back anymore," he said finally.

"Who?" they asked.

"Fritla, the donkey I've been looking for."

They all laughed. "There it is. Look over there."

He took his donkey and went back home, bruised and battered.

The Exploits of Mr. Know-All

[31]

1. The Brother and the Moon

MR. KNOW-ALL was the wisest man in the whole country.[1] He knew everything and could solve all sorts of problems without the slightest reflection. In all kinds of awkward situations, country people resorted to him for help, and they were never disappointed.

During summer and whenever the moon was full, two brothers used to sleep on the roof of the house to get some fresh air. When the moon reached the middle of the sky, it flashed on the forehead of the younger brother and disturbed his sleep. The older brother was worried about this bizarre phenomenon. When he could do nothing to hide the moon from his brother, he went to consult Mr. Know-All. He told him the story and found the answer readily provided: "No problem! When the moon rises tonight, have a loaded rifle beside you. As soon as the moon appears between your brother's eyes, aim the gun and pull the trigger."

---

1. In Moroccan folklore this mythical figure is known as Boumaarif, around whom many anecdotes are invented. This name literally means someone who possesses a lot of knowledge, resembling the famous Juhā.

The following night the older brother kept watch. When the moon appeared on his brother's forehead, he aimed at it and shot. The brother died, and the moon disappeared immediately. They both slept very quietly that night. Next morning the older brother discovered that his brother was dead. He went back to Mr. Know-All weeping.

"Well, that's fate," said Mr. Know-All. "It was written on your brother's forehead."

2. Nomads and Sheep

A group of nomads invaded a plain and let their animals graze there the whole night. Goats were the only livestock they knew; they had never set eyes on any other kind before. Next morning when they woke up, they spotted a flock of white sheep spreading out toward their goats. They were astonished by the appearance of these strange creatures. When they sought an explanation for the riddle, they were directed by a peasant to Mr. Know-All. They explained the problem to him.

"You have to move away," he told them. "These are very dangerous creatures that eat everything, especially goats."

The nomads were very frightened and rushed to pull down their tents. They collected their goats and departed immediately. Actually, the flock of sheep belonged to Mr. Know-All.

3. The Family's Jar

A family kept dried figs in a big jar that had a very narrow mouth to prevent children from stealing the dry fruit. One day a child was hungry and tried to steal a few figs. When he pushed his hand inside, it got stuck and he could not pull it out. When his family arrived and found him in that plight, they did not know how to get his hand out. They thought of breaking the jar, but it was too dear to them. They also thought of cutting the child's hand off, but they could not stand the thought of that, either. The only man who could offer them a decent solution was, of course, Mr. Know-All. They went looking for him, and he listened to their tale.

"It's very simple," he told them. "You want to preserve the jar and you can't cut your child's hand off. So take them both and bury them."

They went back home. When they had dug a grave and were about to bury jar and child, a traveler happened to pass by. When he saw what they were doing, he asked them what the problem was. They explained the situation to him.

"Let me have a try," he said. "Close your eyes and count to one hundred slowly."

When they had shut their eyes, he smashed the jar with his stick, then rode off on his horse. The child cried for joy and started picking up the figs and devouring them. When his family opened their eyes, they saw figs scattered everywhere. They busied themselves picking up the fruit while the child kept laughing.

4. The Willow Tree

A family had a big, tall willow tree that grew in a valley. They decided to cut it down to sell its wood. But felling the tree proved very difficult. They kept going round and round its large trunk until they felt dizzy. Since they had no idea how to handle this awkward situation, they went to Mr. Know-All for a plan. He had a ready answer, of course.

"One of you should climb to the top," he said, "and keep bending it over, and the others should make a big cut in the trunk."

They followed his advice, and the plan worked very well. It did not take them much time to fell the tree. However, the boy who had climbed to the top plunged into a thicket of thorny blackberries. They told him to come out, but he was so entangled that he could not do it. He kept screaming for help. Indeed, the bush was so thorny and dense that no one could get in to pull him out. So once again they went to consult Mr. Know-All.

"Oh, that's much easier," he told them with a laugh. "Set the thicket on fire and get him out."

They did just that and waited until the fire had consumed the entire bush. The family started looking for the boy. When they found him, he was all black but his teeth were grinning as though he were laughing. They were all very angry with him. "Here you are hiding in here and laughing," they yelled at him, "while we've been looking for you!"

He did not answer them. When they finally touched him, he crumbled into ashes.

Glossary

Attoush (dialect): A covered litter or carriage in which a lady is carried on the shoulders or the back of a horse or camel.

Bedouin: A nomadic Arab of the Arabian Peninsula and North Africa.

Boundaf (dialect): A short, tattered gown, usually made of different and old pieces of cloth, worn by poor people.

Burnous: A hooded cloak worn by Arabs.

Couscous (also spelled **kesksu** or **seksu**): A North African dish of granulated wheat, steamed in the vapor of broth or meat.

Fakih: A Muslim scholar who learns the Qur'an and teaches it in a Qur'anic school.

Fritla (local word): Someone who is restless and always slips from grasp.

Fulan (masculine), **Fulana** (feminine): When a person's name is not known, we refer to him or her as "fulan" or "fulana."

Hajj (also **hajji**): The title given to a Muslim who makes a pilgrimage to Mecca.

Hammam: A public bath or Turkish bath.

Hijan (colloquial, unknown origin): A magic box or safe where women usually keep their jewelry.

Jinn (sometimes spelled **djin**): A spirit who inhabits the earth.

Mehras (also **mehraz**): A pestle, a blunt-ended implement for reducing any hard substances to powder by pounding them in a mortar. In popular usage, *mehras* refers to both pestle and mortar.

Mejoun (dialect, unknown origin): A small apparatus that serves for communication, like a mobile phone.

Metmoura (colloquial): An underground stock, a sort of well where peasants store wheat or barley.

Moud (dialect, also **mud**): A measure used especially for grains, a small container made of tin or wood.

Sultan: A king or a Muslim ruler.

Sunna: The official tradition of sayings and deeds of the prophet Muhammad.

Terid (dialect): Thin cakes made of wheat flour, water, oil, and salt butter.

Thasraft (a berber word from Rif, north of Morocco): A *metmoura* or an underground stock.

CRITICAL ANALYSIS BY
Hasan M. El-Shamy

Afterword

Typology

Register of Tale Types

Register of Motifs

Suggested Readings

Afterword

HASAN M. EL-SHAMY

The Present Work

THE SIGNIFICANCE of Professor Jilali El Koudia's anthology of tales is twofold: it is the product of the creative work of two prominent scholars of Arabic literature and it appears in an established series published by a university press with a proven track record for excellence.

The anthology contains thirty-four independent units, all of which are reconstituted and rewritten by El Koudia on the basis of oral renditions of folktales from several of the women in his family.[1] Consequently, the work could be titled "Tales Moroccan Women Told Me" or "Tales I Learned from Moroccan Women."

Noting the rapid disappearance of oral folk narratives from the Moroccan scene, El Koudia states that "[t]he idea behind this book stems from the awareness of this situation and the intention to preserve such lore, hoping that other similar attempts will follow suit. The urgent step

---

1. One source the author cited as "my student Belaali Chakir" is probably male. El Koudia is the collector-narrator-writer of the tales. This re-creative treatment of oral texts has also been adopted by a number of authors dealing with the folk narrative. For a brief description of this approach, see "Folk Narrative Studies in the Arab World," in Hasan M. El-Shamy, "Towards A Demographically Oriented Type Index for Tales of the Arab World," in *Cahiers de Littérature Orale*, no. 23: *La tradition au présent (Monde arabe)*, ed. Praline Gay-Para, (Paris: n.p., 1988), 15–40, esp. 16–20.

to be made is to collect some of these tales, the raw material itself, in order to make them available to future generations."[2]

El Koudia describes the process involved in his re-creation of the texts: "I had to make a selection, discarding repetitions. In fact, the work I have done is more of rewriting, reconstructing the plots, and filling the gaps than just translation. This is because most of my narrators were wordy, repetitive, and kept going back and forth trying to recall the stories from memory."

Available Tale Collections

Morocco has a unique cultural status, with its ethnically and linguistically diverse population; its historical position of leadership in such spheres as politics, arts, and religious movements; its role as a bridge between the Arab-Islamic world and Christian Europe and Muslim Spain (or "al-'Andalus"); and its contacts with sub-Saharan Africa. Interest in Moroccan oral traditional narrative followed the same course as its counterparts in other regions of the Arab world. Apart from narratives that entered classical Arabic literature as part of secondary religious and language sources, interest in the true folktale among the elite was virtually nonexistent. Maghribian traditional cultures and societies have received remarkable attention, primarily from French scholars and their native associates and others with varied religious and political objectives (such as missionaries and colonial administrators with special interests in Berber communities and culture). Their endeavors yielded a rich crop of narrative collections of varying quality, ranging from the scientifically precise to the loosely re-created,[3] that perhaps are unparalleled in any other region of the Arab world.[4]

---

2. The present volume, viii. For available collections from Morocco and other Maghribian communities, see the suggested reading list that follows this afterword. Also, on "preserving" folk traditions, see Hasan M. El-Shamy, "nuzum wa 'ansaq fahrasat al-ma'thur al-sha'bi" (Methods and systems for the classification of folk traditions), al-Ma'thurat al-Sha'biyyah 3, no. 12 (Oct. 1988): 77–109.

3. See Suggested Readings, 182–83.

4. The possible exception is South Arabia, which was studied by a team of scholars from Vienna. See Südarabische Expedition, 10 vols. (Vienna, 1900–1909). However, the interest was not sustained beyond the early 1900s.

On the Tales' Genres

Numerous Maghribian tale collections were presented in terms of their literary genres.[5] A tale's generic qualities are determined according to a number of textual and contextual factors, including form and structure, content, actors (persona), medium of communication, and function or narrator's intent.[6] However, owing to the fact that the tale texts in El Koudia's anthology are re-creations, and that contextual and performance data are not provided (e.g., a narrative is not attributed to a specific narrator, there are no stylized beginnings or endings, or the time and place of narration is not given), the genres of the tales must be inferred primarily on the basis of their content and in light of other versions of the tale in relevant tale collections.

Three texts in the present anthology belong to the "Animal Tale" category;[7] one of these is a simple "animal tale" ("The Mother Goat"),[8] while two texts belong to the animal trickster cycle ("Jackal and Hedgehog" and "Wolf and Hedgehog").

The genre most frequently encountered in the anthology is the Za-

5. For example, Emile Laoust's *Contes berbères du Maroco* classifies the tales in his collection into "contes d'animaux" (nos. 1–34), "contes plaisants" (nos. 35–89), "contes merveilleux" (nos. 90–125), and "legendes hagiograghiquen" (nos. 126–50). In his introduction, he also gives a bibliography (p. xiii), and the Berber names of the ogre and the ogress (p. xvii). Françoise Légey groups the contents of her outstanding anthology, *Contes et légendes populaires du Maroc, recueillis è Marrakech,* into three categories: "contes merveilleux" (nos. 1–57), "contes d'animaux" (nos. 58–74), and "légendes hagiographiques" (nos. 75–93). Jeanne Scelles-Millie's, *Contes arabes du Maghreb* groups her anthology into the six genres: "contes d'animaux," "contes initiatique et romantique," "contes facétieux," "contes moraux," "contes merveilleux," and "contes religieux."

6. See "Classifications of Traditions," in Hasan M. El-Shamy, *Folktales of Egypt: Collected, Translated, and Edited with Middle Eastern and [sub-Saharan] African Parallels* (Chicago: Univ. of Chicago Press, 1980), xliv-xlvi.

7. The classifications are made according to Antti Aarne and Stith Thompson's *The Types of the Folktale: A Classification and Bibliography* (Helsinki: Folklore Fellows Communications, 1964), no. 184.

8. For a text of this tale, see Hasan M. El-Shamy *Tales Arab Women Tell and the Behavioral Patterns They Portray* (Bloomington: Indiana Univ. Press, 1999), 1:63–68.

ubermärchen,[9] typically assigned to female narrators as a culture specialty (*hikayat en-niswan*). These include "Seven Brothers and a Sister,"[10] "The Pigeon Hunter,"[11] "The Fisherman,"[12] "Rhaida,"[13] "The Little Sister with Seven Brothers,"[14] "The Treasure,"[15] "The Jealous Mother,"[16] "Lunja,"[17] "Hdiddan,"[18] "A Tale of Two Women,"[19] "Aamar and His Sister,"[20] "Nunja and the White Dove," [21] "Three Sisters,"[22]

9. Ordinary folktales, "tales of magic," or tales expressing fantasy. They are not taken seriously; they are multi-episodic, adventurous, and full of the magical or the supernatural that is not believed to be true; they use ornate language; and they are told for entertainment. For some native labels for this and other genres in the Arab world, see "Women and the Telling of Fantasy Tales" and "Emergence of Classification of Folk Traditions" in El-Shamy, *Tales Arab Women Tell*, 9–13; also see "Classifications of Traditions," in El-Shamy, *Folktales of Egypt*, xliv-xliv.

10. Type 312A; see appendix, Register of Tale-Types. For a text of this narrative, see El-Shamy, *Tales Arab Women Tell*, 71–72, no. 1–2.

11. For a text of this narrative, see El-Shamy, *Tales Arab Women Tell*, 304–7, no. 40.

12. Ibid., 271–77, no. 34.

13. Ibid., 319–26, no. 46.

14. Ibid., 332–36, no. 47.

15. For a text of this narrative, see Laoust, *Contes berbères du Maroco*, 47, no. 41.

16. For a text of this narrative, see El-Shamy, *Tales Arab Women Tell*, 106–12, no. 8.

17. For a text of this narrative, see El-Shamy, *Folktales of Egypt*, 54–63, no. 8.

18. For Moroccan texts of this narrative, see Légey, *Marrakech*, 139–42, no. 31, and Victorien Loubignac, *Zaër* (Paris, 1952) 1:255–56, no. 10.

19. For a text of this narrative, see El-Shamy, *Folktales of Egypt*, 96–101, no. 14.

20. For a text of this narrative, see El-Shamy, *Tales Arab Women Tell*, résumé 14, "The Girl Who Fed Her Brother the Egg, While She Ate the Shell" 47–48. See type 327A in appendix, Register of Tale-Types.

21. For a text of this narrative, see El-Shamy, *Tales Arab Women Tell*, 255–62, no. 32.

22. For related Moroccan texts, see Emile Laoust, *Contes berbères du Maroco*, 2 vols. (Paris, 1949–50) 191–92, no. 108; and Hans Stumme, *Märchen der Schluh von Tázerwalt* (Leipzig, 1895), 131–46, no. 16.

"Aisha and the Black Cat,"[23] "The Girl in the River,"[24] and "The Modest Girl."[25]

One text, "The Sultan's Daughter,"[26] which deals with jealousy among three sisters, recurs in the oral traditions of the area as a *Zaubermärchen*; however, in the current anthology, the absence of the key motif according to which the sister's lover is a supernatural being invites us to place the text in the romantic/realistic novella category rather than in the magic-tale/fairy tale division. Similarly, the text labeled "Three Women" may be seen as bridging the *Zaubermärchen* and novella categories.

Two texts are of definite novella quality: "Father and Daughters"[27] and "Seven Daughters and Seven Sons."[28]

Two texts are probably local legends, where the event described is assumed to have actually taken place. These are "The Ostrich Hunter" and "The Ghoul and the Cow."

In the division of humorous narratives (jokes, anecdotes, merry tales), two texts stand out: "The Hunter and the Two Partridges" and the four anecdotes that constitute the text titled "A Donkey Named Fritla." The former may be characterized as a "merry tale"—a fairly intricate tale similar to the novella but with humorous content.

Finally, in the category of the "formula tale"—a form of narrating in which the contents are simple and usually subordinated to the form of presentation (performance)—we find two texts; these are "The Spinster Frog" and "M'Hirez the Adopted Child."[29]

23. For a text of this narrative, see El-Shamy, *Tales Arab Women Tell*, 255–62, no. 32.

24. For Moroccan texts of this "Hansel and Gretel" tale-type, see Daisy H. Dwyer, *Images and Self-Images, Male and Female in Morocco* (New York, 1978), 69–70, no. 13, and Albert Socin, "Zum arabischen Dialekt von Marokko," in *Abhandlungen der philologisch-historischen Klasse der königliche Sächsischen Gessellschaft der Wissenschaften zu Leipzig* (Leipzig, 1893), 14:83–85.

25. For a text of this narrative see El-Shamy, *Tales Arab Women Tell*, 255–62, no. 32.

26. Ibid., 262–69, no. 33.

27. Ibid., 159–68, no. 15.

28. Ibid., 113–28, no. 9.

29. For a text of this narrative see El-Shamy, *Tales Arab Women Tell*, 223–28, no. 27.

Notably absent from the anthology are literary tales typically found in scholastic printed sources, a fact that tends to reinforce the argument that oral traditions and written traditions belong to separate cognitive systems.[30] Such narratives include stories from the Arabian Nights, as well as fables (didactic-moralistic brief narratives that often have animals as protagonists and are usually attributed to literary sources such as *Kalilah wa Dimnah*).

The Tales' Contents

A folk narrative may be seen as a description of life and living—real or fictitious.[31] Social relations, especially among family members, constitute the major part of tales. Thus, the nature of feelings among members of the social group that a narrative describes governs the development of the plot. Positive feelings lead to positive results while negative feelings lead to negative outcomes. This principle applies to expressive culture, folk as well as elite, and has been labeled "the structure of sentiments."[32]

In its content the anthology projects a pattern of the structure of sentiments typical of tales found in the Arab world. Perhaps the most salient quality associated with that pattern is the prominence of the brother-

30. See El-Shamy, *Folktales of Egypt*, l-liii, also see Hasan M. El-Shamy "Oral Traditional Tales and the Thousand Nights and a Night: The Demographic Factor," in *The Telling of Stories: Approaches to a Traditional Craft* ed. Morton Nöjgaard et. al. (Odense, Denmark: Odense Univ. Press, 1990), 63–117. The phenomenon harkens back to ancient Egyptian antiquity, where elite scribes seem to reject oral traditions. See Hasan M. El-Shamy, "Introduction to This Edition," in *Popular Stories of Ancient Egypt*, by Sir Gaston C. Maspero; ed. and with an intro. by Hasan El-Shamy. The ABC-CLIO Series of Classic Folk and Fairy Tales, J. Zipes, series ed. (Santa Barbara; Oxford, England: ABC-CLIO), v–xc, especially xxvi–xxx.

31. Hasan M. El-Shamy, *Folk Traditions of the Arab World: A Guide to Motif Classification* (Bloomington: Indiana Univ. Press, 1995), 1:xiii.

32. On the concept of structure of sentiments see Hasan M. El-Shamy, "The Traditional Structure of Sentiments in Mahfouz's Trilogy: A Behavioristic Text Analysis," *Al-'Arabiyya: Journal of the American Association of Teachers of Arabic* 9 (Oct. 1976): 53–74. See also El-Shamy, "Emotionskomponente," *Enzyklopädie des Märchens* (Göttingen) 3, nos. 4–5 (1981), 1391–5.

sister bond.[33] Six texts of El Koudia's anthology revolve around brothers and sisters: "Seven Brothers and a Sister,"[34] "The Pigeon Hunter,"[35] "Rhaida,"[36] "The Little Sister with Seven Brothers,"[37] "Aamar and His Sister,"[38] and "The Girl in the River."[39]

A collateral theme that depicts rivalry among sisters over the same male, who is typically a nonpaternal figure, also occurs in two texts in El Koudia's anthology: "The Sultan's Daughter"[40] and "The Fisherman."[41] The sister-sister rivalry of youth extends into adulthood and characterizes the roles of these siblings in their roles as maternal aunts, each being unkind to her sister's child.[42]

Considering El Koudia's major input and re-creative role in reconstituting and improving the field texts he heard from informants (imperfect as he states these renditions were), it is not easy to determine whether a seemingly idiosyncratic element in a tale is due to a hitherto undiscovered or unrecognized Moroccan cultural trend, or is simply a product of El Koudia's individualistic creative contributions. For example, in the

---

33. See Hasan M. El-Shamy, "The Brother-Sister Syndrome in Arab Family Life. Socio-Cultural Factors in Arab Psychiatry: A Critical Review," *International Journal of Sociology of the Family* (special issue, *The Family in the Middle East*, ed. Mark C. Kennedy) 11, no. 2, (July-Dec. 1981): 313–23.

34. Type 312A; see appendix, Register of Tale-Types. See also note 12, above.

35. Types 312F§ and + 315A; see appendix, Register of Tale-Types. See also note 13, above.

36. Type 313E*; see appendix, Register of Tale-Types. See also note 15, above.

37. Type 451A; see appendix, Register of Tale-Types. For a text of this narrative, see El-Shamy, *Tales Arab Women Tell*, 332–36, no. 47. Also type 872A1§, and for a text of this narrative, see El-Shamy, *Tales Arab Women Tell*, 304–7, no. 40.

38. Type 872A§; see appendix, Register of Tale-Types. Also see note 22, above.

39. Type 327A; see appendix, Register of Tale-Types.

40. Type 432; see appendix, Register of Tale-Types. For a text of this narrative see El-Shamy, *Tales Arab Women Tell*, 262–69, no. 33.

41. For a text of this narrative see El-Shamy, *Tales Arab Women Tell*, 271–77, no. 34.

42. El Koudia, "The Fisherman" [no. 4]; Type: cf. 403D§.

tale "The Pigeon Hunter," a sister initially assumes a heroic role in saving her brother from certain death, a theme that is present in *all* available texts of this tale type. Yet, in an atypical and puzzling development, the same noble sister moves villainously against her brother's fiancée. Besides being incongruent with the assigned social role of a man's sister, this narrative element is unique to El Koudia's text.[43]

Similarly, in the tale titled "The Girl in the River," type 327A, the sister marries on the condition that her brother stays with her. Although this very theme is typical of type 450,[44] no previously recorded text of the tale as it occurs in Morocco contains this element. Likewise, the fact that "A Tale of Two Women,"[45] is told about two female protagonists constitutes a unique phenomenon. Of the forty-nine recorded texts known presently to exist in the Arab world *none* includes this feature.[46] Also, it is not clear whether the dynamic, yet abusive, role the father plays in "The Fisherman," protecting his biological daughter against his own wife, the girl's stepmother,[47] is a genuine new cultural development in Moroccan tales or a creative addition by El Koudia.

Whatever the answers to these questions may be, the anthology as a whole still manifests the traditional structure of sentiments I call "the

43. See Hasan M. El-Shamy, *Brother and Sister. Type 872*: A Cognitive Behavioristic Text Analysis of a Middle Eastern Oikotype* (Folklore Monograph Series, vol. 8, Folklore Publications Group, Bloomington, Indiana), esp. 22–23, 36. For an Algerian Berber text, see El-Shamy, *Tales Arab Women Tell*, 34–307, 448 no. 40.

44. See: Type 450 as it is appended to "Rhaida" [no. 5]. Also see: "Brother Deer" in El-Shamy, *Tales Arab Women Tell*, 293–99, no. 38.

45. Type: 613, *The Two Travelers (Truth and Falsehood)*. [Evil person blinds and mutilates his good-hearted companion (brother)]. For a field text of the tale see: El-Shamy, *Folktales of Egypt*, pp. 96–101, no. 14.

46. See Hasan M. El-Shamy, " 'Noble and Vile' or 'Genuine and False'? Some Linguistic and Typological Comments on *Folktales of Egypt*," in *Fabula. Zeitschrift für Erzählforschung* 24, nos. 3–4 (Berlin and New York, 1983): 341–46. The full documentation will be available in Hasan M. El-Shamy, *Types of the Folktale in the Arab World: A Demographically Oriented Tale-Type Index* (Bloomington: Indiana Univ. Press, forthcoming).

47. Mot. T205.1§, "Wife-beating." Compare the passive role of the father in "The Fisherman's Daughter," in *Tales Arab Women Tell*, 271–77, no. 34; Mot. P200.0.2.1§, "Father is powerless."

brother-sister syndrome," which is shown to underlie such diverse literary works as Naguib Mahfouz's trilogy[48] and *Tales Arab Women Tell*.

Lore in Literature

Whether acknowledged or not, "no person is lore-free."[49] Lore reaches a
child early in life and leaves an indelible lifelong impression. Thus, it has
been stated:

> Before being introduced at school to elite "poetry," the child will already
> have acquired a deep sense of the poetic from mother's lullabies and
> children's rhymes chanted during play or tale-telling sessions. . . . And
> before being schooled in the novel or short story (borrowed recently
> from the West), he or she will have developed a deep sense of "story"
> from repeated immersions in folk narration. These immersions occur in
> a relaxed atmosphere of security, trust, and acceptance—an affective
> state that tends to accompany tale-telling for the rest of the listener's
> life.[50]

The extent to which elite writers (poets, novelists, etc.) have employed
oral lore in their creative products has been quite diverse, ranging from
mere citing of a folk formulaic statement, such as a proverb or proverbial
simile, lullaby, or the like, to the adoption of an entire oral tale plot.
Such is the case, for example, with some of the works of Tawfiq al-Hakim,
one of Egypt's early prominent and honored novelists and playwrights. In
his *Yawmiyyat na'ib fi al-aryaf*, numerous folk motifs are cited; one of
these is part of a peasant song extolling a maiden's "long eyelash that
could cover an acre of farmland."[51] Conversely, he adopted an entire tale
plot[52] and gave it an elite literary dressing in the form of a short drama

48. "The Traditional Structure of Sentiments in Mahfouz's Trilogy," 53–74.

49. Hasan M. El-Shamy, "Psychologically-based Criteria for Classification by
Motif and Tale-Type" *Journal of Folklore Research* 34, no. 3 (1997), 233–43. esp.
233.

50. El-Shamy *Tales Arab Women Tell*, 6.

51. Designated as new Mot. F541.14.1.1§, ‡"Eyelashes that would cover an
acre."

52. Type 1534; see appendix, Register of Tale Types. For a text of this narrative, see *Folktales of Egypt*, 209–12, no. 54.

that maintained all the characteristics of the oral text except for language and the extended dialogues. Al-Hakim, a Cairene, stated that he heard the story during his childhood and that it is "reminiscent of some [current] international events."[53]

In addition to these overt facets of cultural expressions, another covert dimension comprising a network of acquired affective experiences of love, hate, fear, admiration, and resentment (i.e., sentiments) is always present.

When applied to Mahfouz's trilogy (*Bayna al-qasryn, Qasr al-shawq,* and *al-Sukkariyyah*) where the author plays the role of the boy Kamal, the youngest of three brothers and two sisters—the younger of whom he loved—the brother-sister bond permeated the entire work from beginning to end, spanning three generations and covering some 1,500 pages. Furthermore, it was shown that the structure of sentiments in the trilogy is identical with the structure of sentiments in a folktale known across the Arab world, including Morocco: Type 872*/872§, *Brother and Sister.* The likely sources from which Mahfouz acquired his sense of the traditional structure of sentiments and "story" are his traditional Egyptian environment, his mother, and an old servant woman named Umm Hanafi.

Some critics unfamiliar with Egyptian folklore attributed various aspects of the trilogy to Western philosophies or European literary trends. This point of view was shown to be stereotypical and inaccurate. Thus, it has been stated:

> Whatever effect the European schools might have had on Mahfouz's *Trilogy,* their influence by no means amounts to the impact of Egyptian lore. Perhaps it would be more appropriate to seek Mahfouz's literary roots in the folk narrative repertoires of his mother and the old family servant Umm Hanafi, his two raconteurs. . . . Perhaps they did fill Kamal's [Mahfouz's] head with "medieval superstitions," . . . but in addition they instilled into him the forms and contents of his thoughts, feelings and expressions.[54]

53. Tawfiq al-Hakim, "The Judge and the Baker," *al-Ahram* (Cairo) (June 12, 1970), 6–7. See also *Folktales of Egypt,* 279.

54. El-Shamy, "The Traditional Structure of Sentiments in Mahfouz's *Trilogy,*" 68–69.

In the present case, it would be safe to assume that El Koudia's mother, sister, wife, mother-in-law, and niece have had a similar effect on his worldview and artistic repertoire, including the centrality of a sister in a brother's life (and vice versa). Perhaps elite Arabic literature will soon see a major work by El Koudia reflecting the contents of the minds, hearts, and souls of his own sources of Moroccan lore, who inspired this literary anthology of retold tales.

Typology

Typological Tools

THE PRESENT IDENTIFICATIONS include two classificatory concepts: "tale type," and "motif."[1]

Simply stated, a tale type is a full narrative that recurs cross-culturally; a "subtype" is a recurrent variation on a tale type (or a tale's plot) that may characterize a certain social group on the basis of age, gender, ethnicity, location, or occupation. Meanwhile, a motif denotes a smaller narrative unit recurrent in folk literature; according to S. Thompson, motifs are "those details out of which full-fledged narratives are composed."[2] It should be pointed out that both concepts are not ends in themselves but tools to assist researchers in locating parallels and counterparts of certain data (tales or themes/motifs) for the purpose of conducting objective research.

1. See Antti Aarne and Stith Thompson, *The Types of the Folktale: A Classification and Bibliography* (Helsinki, Folklore Fellows Communications, no. 184, 1961, 1964). See also Hasan El-Shamy, "Nuzum wa 'ansaq fahrasat al-ma'thur al-sha'bi" (Methods and systems for the classification of folk traditions). In *al-Ma'thurat al-Sha'biyyah* 3, no. 12 (Oct. 1988), 77–109.

2. Stith Thompson, *Motif-Index of Folk Literature* (Bloomington: Indiana Univ. Press, 1955–58), 1:10; see also Hasan El-Shamy, "Psychologically-Based Criteria for Classification by Motif and Tale-Type," *Journal of Folklore Research* 34, no. 3 (1997): 233–43.

A tale type is designated by an Arabic number that may *end with* a letter to indicate that it is a subtype or a variation on a cardinal tale type (e.g. 312F§, 510A); meanwhile a motif is designated by a letter indicating its general nature within Thompson's motif schema followed by a number (e.g., B17.1.5.1§, Z71.5.1). Most oral tales incorporate a limited number of tale types; however, a tale may contain dozens of motifs.

Unfortunately, with reference to Arabic-Islamic traditions, both the types of the folktale and the motif index as they stand now are woefully inadequate both in terms of inclusion of available data, and in recognition of culture-specific concepts and social practices.[3] I have developed two new reference works to address Arab-world traditions more precisely. These are Hasan El-Shamy, *Folk Traditions of the Arab World: A Guide to Motif Classification*, 2 vols. (Bloomington: Indiana Univ. Press, 1995); and *Types of the Folktale in the Arab World: A Demographically Oriented Tale-Type Index for the Arab World* (Indiana Univ. Press, forthcoming).

All *new* tale types added to the Aarne-Thompson tale-type system, and new motifs added to the Thompson motif system, are signaled by a section mark (§) at the end of the number. A double dagger (‡) indicates a *newer* tale type or motif, developed or added after the publication of *Folk Traditions of the Arab World* in 1995; see Appendix 1, "Locations of Tale-Types in the Arab World," vol. 1, 415–42 in that work.

Tale Types and Select Motifs in El Koudia's *Moroccan Folktales*

Seven Brothers and a Sister [no. 1] (*Zaubermärchen*)
    Type: 312A. *The Brother Rescues His Sister from the Tiger [(Hyena, Ogre, etc.).]*
        Z71.5.1. Seven brothers and one sister.
        B17.1.5.1§. Hostile (mischievous) cat extinguishes fire by urinating on it.
        K477.0.1.1.1.1§. ‡Angry person (animal) deprives household of use of fire by extinguishing its source (wetting matches, or the like).

3. For some of remarks on these shortcomings see "The Aarne-Thompson Type Index and Egyptian Folktales," in H. El-Shamy, *Folktales of Egypt*, p. 237; see also "General Remarks," in El-Shamy, *Folk Traditions of the Arab World: A Guide to Motif Classification* (Bloomington: Indiana Univ. Press, 1995) 1:xiii-xiv.

+ Type: 363. *The Vampire* (Pt.).

G412.4§. ‡Person falls into ogre's (ogress's) power when he goes to the predator's dwelling seeking help (usually to borrow household article: fire, salt, sieve, etc.).

E251.3.3. Vampire sucks blood.

M341.2.19. Prophecy: death at hands of certain person.

N331.1.5.2§. ‡Object carried by flying bird (or airplane) drops and kills person (animal).

Z292.0.1.1§. ‡Tragic ending of a story (tale): all die.

The Pigeon Hunter [no. 2] (*Zaubermärchen*)

Type: 312F§. *Sister Rescues Infant (Fetus) Brother with Help from Kindly Animal.* Escape from cruel father, pregnant mother killed by animals, fetus (brother) raised by little sister.

B450. Helpful birds.

P771.3§. ‡Goods for services.

K2212.2.2§. ‡Treacherous husband's sister: plots against her brother's wife (fiancée).

P264.4§. Inherent rivalry between a man's sister and his future wife (fiancée, sweetheart, etc.).

+ Type: 315A. *The Cannibal Sister.* [Destroys community and tries to devour her brother.]

K2212.0.2. Treacherous sister as mistress of robber (giant) plots against brother.

B515. Resuscitation by animals.

The Sultan's Daughter [no. 3] (*Zaubermärchen*/novella—lost magic component)

Type: 432. *The Prince as Bird.* [In form of snake (serpent), he visits heroine and is wounded by her jealous sisters.]

P252.2. Three sisters.

W195.3§. Being loved (favored) within family envied.

P426.2.1.2§. ‡Person disappointed with social life becomes hermit (anchorite, ascetic, etc.).

T11.1. Love from mere mention or description.

K1349.8.1§. ‡Entrance into maiden's room through secret passage (tunnel, hole in wall, etc.).

cf. K1523. Underground passage [(tunnel)] to paramour's house. (Inclusa.) Woman goes from one to the other.

U194.2§. ‡Rumors spread quickly.

F721.1.0.1§. ‡Crystal (glass) tunnel.

W181 Jealousy.

W195.9.3§. Sister envies sister's handsome husband (suitor, lover).

W179.1§. ‡Power of hatred (envy, jealousy, malice, etc.).

+ Type: 879:IV. *The Sugar Puppet.* (As fin.)

The Fisherman [no. 4] (*Zaubermärchen*)

Type: 510A. *Cinderella.* [Girl persecuted by stepmother and stepsisters is aided by fairy.]

M250.1§. ‡Deathbed wish: dying person (father, mother, husband, wife, etc.) makes a wish.

H501.4§. ‡Test of reaching puberty (physical development, i.e., maturation).

K289§. Artificial (deceptive) compliance: one party to a bargain arranges for the terms (conditions, stipulations) to occur.

B375.1. Fish returned to water: grateful.

B80.0.1§. ‡Fish-man (merman, mermaid) as helper.

P200.0.1.2.1§. ‡Father protects children against stepmother (his wife).

cf. T205.1§. Wife-beating.

J1141.1.19.1§. ‡Confession sought or obtained by torture.

+ Type: cf. 403D§. *The Cruel Maternal Aunt Blinds Her Niece and Substitutes Her Own Daughter as Bride.*

D582. Transformation by sticking magic pin into head.

D154.2. ‡Transformation: man to pigeon.

Q411.4. Death as punishment for treachery.

Rhaida [no. 5] (*Zaubermärchen*)

Type: 313E*. *Girl Flees from Brother Who Wants to Marry Her.*

P253.0.2. ‡One sister and two brothers.

N365.3.3§. Boy finds a woman's hair and decides to marry the person to whom it belongs: it is his sister's.

K778. Capture through the wiles of a woman.

P550.1§. ‡War.

Q242.7§. ‡Brother's incestuous desire with his sister punished.

Q552.3.3. ‡Drought as punishment.

+ Type: 450. *Little Brother and Little Sister*. [They flee from home; brother transformed into deer, sister nearly murdered by jealous rivals.]

P250.0.1.3§. ‡Brother and sister undergo similar experiences.

D555.3§. ‡Transformation by drinking from well (spring).

The Little Sister with Seven Brothers [no. 6] (*Zaubermärchen*)

Type: 451A. *The Sister Seeking Her Nine Brothers*. [Change of color (race): slave-girl as substitute sister.]

P253.0.1.2§. ‡Brother(s) need(s) a sister (be born).

+ Type: 872A1§. *Snakes in the Sister's Belly*: treacherous brother's wife (brothers' wives).

+ Type: 285B*. *Snake Enticed Out of Man's Stomach*. Patient fed salt: animal comes out for water.

The Treasure [no. 7] (*Zaubermärchen*/humor.)

Type: 564. *The Magic Providing Purse and "Out, Boy, Out of the Sack!"* [Magic objects usurped, recovered via another object.]

B103.2.1. Treasure-laying bird.

D881.2. Recovery of magic object by use of magic cudgel.

Father and Daughters [no. 8] (Novella)

Type: 879. *The Basil Maidens (The Sugar Puppet, Viola)*. [Daughters of poor vendor match wits with prince.]

+ Type: 884B*. *Girl Dressed as a Man Deceives the King*.

H1578. Test of sex [(gender)]: to discover person masking as of another sex.

+ Type: 883§. *Innocent Slandered (Suspected) Female*. (General.)

P253.1.1§. Brother as guardian of his sister's chastity (sexual honor).

P253.1.1.1§. Brother is to execute his sister; he is compassionate: spares her life.

cf. K512. Compassionate executioner. A servant charged with killing the hero (heroine) arranges the escape of the latter.

H51. Recognition by scar.

The Jealous Mother [no. 9] (*Zaubermärchen*)
Type: 709. *Snow-White*. [Mother jealous of her daughter's beauty.]
K477.0.1.1.1.1§. ‡Angry person (animal) deprives household of use of fire by extinguishing its source (wetting matches, or the like).
K2251.1. Treacherous slave-girl.
E251.3.3. Vampire sucks blood.
N888.1§. ‡Helper belonging to adversary religious persuasion.

Seven Daughters and Seven Sons [no. 10] (Novella)
Type: 923C§. *Girl Wins Against Boy (Usually, Her Eldest Paternal Cousin) in a Contest of Worth.*
J1111. Clever girl.
J1129§. Female trickster.
K99.1.1§. ‡Contest in commercial prowess won by deception.
+ Type: cf. 676. *Open Sesame.* [Ali Baba and the Forty Thieves: the rich but unkind brother imitates; he is killed.]

Lunja [no. 11] (*Zaubermärchen*)
Type: 310A§. *The Maiden in the Tower: Louliyyah.* Youth cursed to fall in love with ogre's (ogress's, witch's) daughter: elopement, transformation (separation), and disenchantment (reunion).
G443§. Ogre adopts human child.
+ Type: 1643A§. *Bird (Beast) with Man in Belly Captured by Setting Out More Meat (Grain).*
F913.4§. Eagle with man in its belly fed much meat: too heavy to fly and victim is rescued;
+ Type: 533A§. *Beautiful Maiden in Hideous Disguise.* She is detected by the prince (Khushayshibun, Khashaban, Galadanah, Gulaidah, etc.).

Hdiddan [no. 12] (*Zaubermärchen*)
Type: 327B. *The Dwarf and the Giant.* [Nuss-Nusais, Hdaydun, etc.]
F771.1.4. ‡Steel [(iron)] castle (house).
K741.1. Capture by tarring [(placing gum on)] back of horse.
+ Type: 837A§. *The Evil Counsel (Remedy): Applied to Counselor.*
+ Type: 122F. *"Wait Till I Am Fat Enough."* [Captive escapes.]

K1941. Disguised flayer. An imposter dresses in the skin of his victim.

+ Type: 1121. *Ogre's Wife Burned in His Own Oven.*

A Tale of Two Women [no. 13] (*Zaubermärchen*)

Type: 613. *The Two Travelers (Truth and Falsehood).* [Evil person blinds and mutilates his good-hearted companion (brother).]

W171.0.2§. ‡"To be of two intents: [a declared good one and a harbored evil (malicious) one]." (*Abu-niyyatain*).

Z121.0.1.1§. ‡Honest intentions personified (*"Niyyah Salimah"*).

Z127.0.3.1§. ‡Dishonest intentions personified (*"Niyyah Su'"*).

K231.1.1.2. Mutual agreement to divide [(share)] food. Trickster eats other's food and then refuses to divide his own.

M225. Eyes exchanged for food.

F1045. Night spent in tree.

B513. Remedy learned from overhearing animal meeting.

cf. D926. Magic well.

D2161.3.1.1. Eyes torn out magically replaced.

F952. Blindness miraculously cured.

Aamar and His Sister [no. 14] (*Zaubermärchen*)

Type: 872A§. *The Pregnancy of the Virgin Sister by Treachery.*

S301. Children abandoned (exposed).

T131.11.1§. Descent (ancestry) as obstacle to marriage.

+T121.8.2§. ‡Man (youth) of respectable social rank weds lowly girl (vagabond, beggar, etc.).

+ Type: 872E§. *The Sister Is Accused of Murdering Her Brother's Son and Is Mutilated.* (Her hands cut off, but she is subsequently vindicated.)

+ Type: 706:pt. *The Maiden Without Hands.* [Severed hands restored.]

Q552.2.3.5§. ‡Treacherous (guilty) person sinks into earth (swallowed by earth).

Q414. Punishment: burning alive.

Three Women [no. 15] (*Zaubermärchen*/novella)

Type: 707C§. *Infants Cast Away, (by Jealous Co-wife, Mother-in-law, Slave, etc.), and Subsequently Reunited with Their Parents.*

K2116.1.1.1. Innocent woman accused of eating her new-born children.

H51.1. Recognition by birthmark.

S117. ‡Death by dragging behind horse.

cf. Q416. Punishment: drawing asunder by horses.

Nunja and the White Dove [no. 16] (*Zaubermärchen*)

Type: 511. *One-Eye, Two-Eyes, Three-Eyes.* [Stepsister and her brother spy on heroine.]

E607.1. Bones of dead collected and buried. Return in another form directly from grave.

B391. Animal grateful for food.

P771.3.1§. ‡Food for a service (e.g., ear of corn for a shave, an egg for knife sharpening, and the like).

+ Type: 510. *Cinderella and Cap o' Rushes.*

+ Type: 403C. *The Witch Secretly Substitutes Her Own Daughter* for the bride. [Substitute bride thrown under bridge; reed grows out of her navel].

G61. Relative's flesh eaten unwittingly.

The Ghoul and the Cow [no. 17] (Probably local legend)

+ Type: cf. 311C§. *The Father Rescues His Abducted Daughter from Magician (Ogre, Witch)*

G412.3§. ‡Ogre's (ogress's) fire lures person.

R153.3. Father rescues son(s).

J226.8§. ‡Choice: to save a person or goods (e.g., son or cow, wife or her jewelry, etc.).

The Ostrich Hunter [no. 18] (Probably local legend)

No tale type

K1823.0.4§. ‡Disguise as animal (bird) so as to hunt (catch game: bird or animal).

L406§. Hunter (predator) becomes hunted (prey).

cf. N338. Death as result of mistaken identity: wrong person killed.

Jackal and Hedgehog [no. 19] (Animal/trickster)

Type: 59**§. *Tricks and Countertricks: Two Animals Make Trouble for Each Other*. Series of tricky adventures; (the jackal and the hedgehog).

J1117.4§. Hedgehog (porcupine) as trickster.

K2400§. ‡Deception for deception (tit for tat): deceived person gets even in a like manner (same ruse, strategy, trick, etc.).

+ Type: cf. 4. *Carrying the Sham-Sick Trickster*. [Fox feigns illness and rides on dupe's back.]

+ Type: cf. 223. *The Bird and the Jackal as Friends*. [By feigning illness, confederates help each other steal food (or play tricks on others).]

+ Type: 21. *Eating His Own Entrails*. The fox persuades the Wolf (bear) to do so.

K1020. Deception into disastrous attempt to procure food.

K1025.3§. ‡Trickster pretends to produce strips of meat from own body: foolish imitator dies attempting to do the same.

Wolf and Hedgehog [no. 20] (Animal/trickster)

Type: 59**§. *Tricks and Countertricks: Two Animals Make Trouble for Each Other*. Series of Tricky Adventures; (the Jackal and the Hedgehog).

J1117.4§. Hedgehog (porcupine) as trickster.

+ Type: 32. *The Wolf Descends into the Well in One Bucket and Rescues the Fox in the Other*.

+ Type: 41*. *Fox in the Orchard*. [He overeats in the vineyard: must fast to be able to exit.]

+ Type: 33*. *Fox Overeats in Cellar;* thrown on dunghill and escapes [by feigning death].

+ Type: 47A. *The Fox (Bear, etc.) Hangs by His Teeth to the Horse's Tail[:] Hare's Lip*.

The Hunter and the Two Partridges [no. 21] (Merry tale)

Type: 1741. *The Priest's Guests and the Eaten Chickens*. ["Pair" of chickens which were to be had for dinner hidden, guest induced to flee for fear of losing a 'pair' of his body parts and is chased].

J1563.5. Guest frightened away by housewife [(host's wife)].

cf. K2137.1§. "Both are yours, if you catch me!" The husband is made by his faithless wife to believe that his guest has fled with "both" geese, and guest that husband is after his testicles. A chase ensues: husband: "Give me one." Guest retorts.

Three Sisters [no. 22] (*Zaubermärchen*)
   Type: cf. 327. *The Children and the Ogre*.
   + Type: cf. 327L§. *Fleeing Sisters Possess Ogress's (Supernatural Cat's) Treasure*.
      S11.1.2§. Cruel father exposes daughter(s).
      T115.2§. ‡Woman (girl) marries ogre.
      L432.2. Impoverished father begs from daughter he has banished: recognized.
      Q291.3§. ‡Hard-hearted parent(s) punished.
      Q440.1§. ‡Punishment: expulsion from family (person disowned, disinherited).
      P788.1§. ‡Excessive shame (dishonor, disgrace: '*ar, khizy*) from violation of mores.

Aisha and the Black Cat [no. 23] (*Zaubermärchen*)
   Type: 480. *The Spinning Women by the Spring. The Kind and Unkind Girls*. [Ogress rewards the kind stepsister and punishes the unkind.]
      Q40. Kindness rewarded.
      Q280. Unkindness punished.
      F401.3.6.1§. Spirit (afrit, jinni) in the form of cat.

The Spinster Frog [no. 24] (Formula)
   Type: 2028B§. *She-Mouse Seeks a Husband*
   + Type: cf. 103A1§. *Beetle (Ant, Locust, Bird, etc.) as the Mouse's Unhappy Wife*. Attempts at mediation.
      N102.1§. Woman (girl) luckless in spite of beauty, virtue, and wealth.

The Girl in the River [no. 25] (*Zaubermärchen*)
   Type: 327A. *Hansel and Gretel*. [Brother and sister triumph over witch (ogress).]
      R135.1. Crumb (grain) trail eaten by birds.
      G512.3. ‡Ogre burned to death.
      P254.0.1§. ‡Household composed of only brother and sister(s). They live alone in palace (house, cave, etc.).

R351.0.1§. Maiden in tree discovered by her reflection in water.

T52.10.1§. ‡Girl will marry with a stipulation.

T52.11.1§. Sister marries to save brother(s).

M'Hirez the Adopted Child [no. 26] (Formula)

Type: cf. 2021*. *The Louse Mourns Her Spouse, the Flea.*

Type: cf. 2022. *The Death of the Little Hen Described with Unusual Words.*

T670.1§. ‡Childless couple adopt child.

cf. L111.4.4. Mistreated orphan hero.

P272. Foster mother.

P272.0.1§. ‡Treacherous foster mother.

K2127. ‡False accusation of theft.

B299.5.1. Animal mutilates self to express sympathy.

F819§. ‡Sympathetic plant(s).

S110.0.2§. Suicide intended (attempted).

The Girl and the Fakih [no. 27] (Novella/probably local legend)

Type: cf. 896. *The Lecherous Holy Man and the Maiden in a Box.* (Seeks revenge when he fails to seduce girl left in his trust).

K2284. Treacherous priest [(cleric, sheik, *mulla*)].

P426.0.8§. ‡Immoral (corrupt) cleric.

Z88§. ‡Sarcasm.

T160.0.3§. Publication of defloration: blood displayed.

+ Type: cf. 879:IV. *The Sugar Puppet.*

F1041.21.9.1§. Death from shame (humiliation).

The Modest Girl [no. 28] (*Zaubermärchen*)

Type: 480. *The Spinning Women by the Spring. The Kind and Unkind Girls.* [Ogress rewards the kind stepsister and punishes the unkind.]

K235.2.2§. ‡Bag of gold (silver) expected, but bag of scorpions (snakes) received.

The Mother Goat [no. 29] (Animal tale)

Type: 123. *The Wolf and the Kids.* [Mother goat rescues her young from predator.]

P200.1.1§. "Mother as head of single-parent family."

P209.1§. "Mother as provider."

cf. F913. "Victims rescued from swallower's belly."

A Donkey Named Fritla [no. 30] (Humor/anecdote)
 Type: 1696. *What Should I Have Said (Done)?* [Literal following of in-
 structions lead to comic results.]
  D1812.5.1. Bad omens.
  N120.2§. ‡Name (word, statement, etc.) harbinger of evil.
  N134.0.1§. Person brings good luck.

The Exploits of Mr. Know-All: The Brother and Moon [no. 31.1]
(Humor/anecdote)
 Type: 1228B§. *Shooting at a Pest Alighted on Animal: Hitting the
 Animal.*
  J1215§. ‡Know-all person ("*Abu-el-'Urraif*"): a talkative fool.
  J1833.2§. ‡Shooting (striking) at a pest (bird, insect) alighted on
  animal's horn (back): hitting animal.
  N331.1.5§. ‡Object (rock, shoe, knife, projectile, etc.) thrown
  causes unintentional killing.
  S73.1. Fratricide.

The Exploits of Mr. Know-All: Nomads and Sheep [no. 31.2]
(Humor/anecdote)
 No tale-type
  J1215§. ‡Know-all person ("*Abu-el-'Urraif*"): a talkative fool.
  J2624. Fright at animals' eyes in the dark.
  cf. J758. Beware of following an interested adviser.

The Exploits of Mr. Know-All: The Family's Jar [no. 31.3]
(Humor/anecdote)
 Type: cf. 1294A*. *Child with Head Caught in Jar.* [Head is to be cut
 off].
  J1215§. ‡Know-all person ("*Abu-el-'Urraif*"): a talkative fool.

The Exploits of Mr. Know-All: The Willow Tree [no. 31.4]
(Humor/anecdote)
 Type: cf. 1241. *The Tree Is to be Pulled Down* in order to give it water
 to drink.
  J1215§. ‡Know-all person ("*Abu-el-'Urraif*"): a talkative fool.
  J2199. ‡Absurd shortsightedness—miscellaneous.

Register of Tale Types

Numbers in brackets refer to tale numbers in *Moroccan Folktales*.

Animal Tales

4   *Carrying the Sham-Sick Trickster*. [Fox feigns illness and rides on dupe's back] [no. 19]

21   *Eating His Own Entrails*. The fox persuades the wolf (bear) to do so [no. 19]

32   *The Wolf Descends into the Well in One Bucket and Rescues the Fox in the Other* [no. 20]

41*   *Fox in the Orchard*. [He overeats in the vineyard: must fast to be able to exit] [no. 20]

47A   *The Fox (Bear, etc.) Hangs by His Teeth to the Horse's Tail[:] Hare's Lip* [no. 20]

59**§   *Tricks and Countertricks: Two Animals Make Trouble for Each Other*. Series of tricky adventures; (the jackal and the hedgehog) [nos. 19, 20]

103A1§   *Beetle (Ant, Locust, Bird, etc.) as the Mouse's Unhappy Wife*. Attempts at mediation [no. 24]

122F   *"Wait Till I Am Fat Enough."* [Captive escapes] [no. 12]

123   *The Wolf and the Kids*. [Mother goat rescues her young from predator] [no. 29]

223   *The Bird and the Jackal as Friends*. [By feigning illness, confed-

erates help each other steal food (or play tricks on others)] [no. 19]

285B*   *Snake Enticed Out of Man's Stomach.* Patient fed salt: animal comes out for water [no. 6]

Ordinary Folktales

310A§   *The Maiden in the Tower: Louliyyah.* Youth cursed to fall in love with ogre's (ogress', witch's) daughter: elopement, transformation (separation), and disenchantment (reunion) [no. 11]

311C§   *The Father Rescues His Abducted Daughter from Magician (Ogre, Witch)* [no. 17]

312A   *The Brother Rescues His Sister from the Tiger [(Hyena, Ogre, etc.)]* [no. 1]

312F§   *Sister Rescues Infant (Fetus) Brother with Help from Kindly Animal.* Escape from cruel father, pregnant mother killed by animals, fetus (brother) raised by little sister [no. 2]

313E*   *Girl Flees from Brother Who Wants to Marry Her* [no. 5]

315A   *The Cannibal Sister.* [Destroys community and tries to devour her brother] [no. 2]

327   *The Children and the Ogre* [no. 22]

327A   *Hansel and Gretel.* [Brother and sister triumph over witch (ogress)] [no. 25]

327B   *The Dwarf and the Giant.* [Nuss-Nusais, Hdaydun, etc.] [no. 12]

327L§   *Fleeing Sisters Possess Ogress's (Supernatural Cat's) Treasure* [no. 22]

33*   *Fox Overeats in Cellar;* thrown on dunghill and escapes [by feigning death] [no. 20]

363   *The Vampire* (pt.) [no. 1]

403C   *The Witch Secretly Substitutes Her Own Daughter* for the bride. [Substitute bride thrown under bridge; reed grows out of her navel] [no. 16]

403D§   *The Cruel Maternal Aunt Blinds Her Niece and Substitutes Her Own Daughter as Bride* [no. 4]

432   *The Prince as Bird.* [In form of snake (serpent), he visits heroine and is wounded by her jealous sisters] [no. 3]

450   *Little Brother and Little Sister.* [They flee from home; brother

transformed into deer, sister nearly murdered by jealous rivals] [no. 5]

451A   *The Sister Seeking Her Nine Brothers.* [Change of color (race): slave-girl as substitute sister] [no. 6]

480   *The Spinning Women by the Spring. The Kind and Unkind Girls.* [Ogress rewards the kind stepsister and punishes the unkind]. [Nos. 23, 28]

510   *Cinderella and Cap o' Rushes* [no. 16]

510A   *Cinderella.* [Girl persecuted by stepmother and stepsisters is aided by fairy] [no. 4]

511   *One-Eye, Two-Eyes, Three-Eyes.* [Stepsister and her brother spy on heroine] [no. 16]

533A§   *Beautiful Maiden in Hideous Disguise.* She is detected by the prince. (Khushayshibun, Khashaban, Galadanah, Gulaidah, etc.) [no. 11]

564   *The Magic Providing Purse and "Out, Boy, Out of the Sack!".* [[Magic objects usurped, recovered via another object] [no. 7]

613   *The Two Travelers (Truth and Falsehood).* [Evil person blinds and mutilates his good-hearted companion (brother)] [no. 13]

676   *Open Sesame.* [Ali Baba and the Forty Thieves: the rich but unkind brother imitates; he is killed] [no. 10]

706   *The Maiden Without Hands.* [Severed hands restored] [no. 14]

707C§   *Infants Cast Away (by Jealous Co-wife, Mother-in-law, Slave, etc.), and Subsequently Reunited with Their Parents* [no. 15]

709   *Snow-White.* [Mother jealous of her daughter's beauty] [no. 9]

837A§   *The Evil Counsel (Remedy): Applied to Counselor* [no. 12]

872A1§   *Snakes in the Sister's Belly:* treacherous brother's wife (brothers' wives) [no. 6]

872A§   *The Pregnancy of the Virgin Sister by Treachery* [no. 14]

872E§   *The Sister Is Accused of Murdering Her Brother's Son and Is Mutilated.* (Her hands cut off, but she is subsequently vindicated) [no. 14]

879   *The Basil Maidens (The Sugar Puppet, Viola).* [Daughters of poor vendor match wits with prince] [no. 8]

879:IV   *The Sugar Puppet.* (As fin.) [nos. 3, 27]

883§   *Innocent Slandered (Suspected) Female.* (General) [no. 8]

884B*   *Girl Dressed as a Man Deceives the King* [no. 8]

896   *The Lecherous Holy Man and the Maiden in a Box.* (Seeks revenge when he fails to seduce girl left in his trust) [no. 27]

923C§   *Girl Wins Against Boy (Usually Her Eldest Paternal Cousin) in a Contest of Worth* [no. 10]

1121   *Ogre's Wife Burned in His Own Oven* [no. 12]

Jokes and Anecdotes

1228B§   *Shooting at a Pest Alighted on Animal: Hitting the Animal* [no. 31.1]

1241   *The Tree Is to Be Pulled Down* in order to give it water to drink [no. 31.4]

1294A*   *Child with Head Caught in Jar.* [Head is to be cut off] [no. 31.3]

1534   *Series of Clever Unjust Decisions.* [Dishonest judge misapplies law] [see Afterword, n. 53]

1643A§   *Bird (Beast) with Man in Belly Captured by Setting Out More Meat (Grain)* [no. 11]

1696   *What Should I Have Said (Done)?* [Literal following of instructions lead to comic results] [no. 30]

1741   *The Priest's Guests and the Eaten Chickens.* ["Pair" of chickens which were to be had for dinner hidden, guest induced to flee for fear of losing a "pair" of his body parts and is chased] [no. 21]

Formula Tales

2021*   *The Louse Mourns Her Spouse, the Flea* [no. 26]

2022   *The Death of the Little Hen Described with Unusual Words* [no. 26]

2028B§   *She-Mouse Seeks a Husband* [no. 24]

Register of Motifs

Numbers in brackets refer to tale numbers in *Moroccan Folktales*.

B. Animals

B17.1.5.1§	Hostile (mischievous) cat extinguishes fire by urinating on it [no. 1]
B80.0.1§	‡Fish-man (merman, mermaid) as helper [no. 4]
B103.2.1	Treasure-laying bird [no. 7]
B299.5.1	Animal mutilates self to express sympathy [no. 26]
B375.1	Fish returned to water: grateful [no. 4]
B391	Animal grateful for food [no. 16]
B450	Helpful birds [no. 2]
B513	Remedy learned from overhearing animal meeting [no. 13]
B515	Resuscitation by animals [no. 2]

D. Magic [and Similar Supernatural Occurrences]

D154.2	‡Transformation: man to pigeon [no. 4]
D555.3§	‡Transformation by drinking from well (spring) [no. 5]
D582	Transformation by sticking magic pin into head [no. 4]
D881.2	Recovery of magic object by use of magic cudgel [no. 7]
D926	Magic well [no. 13]

D1812.5.1	Bad omens [no. 30]
D2161.3.1.1	Eyes torn out magically replaced [no. 13]

E. The Dead

E251.3.3	Vampire sucks blood [nos. 1, 9]
E607.1	Bones of dead collected and buried. Return in another form directly from grave [no. 16]

F. Marvels

F401.3.6.1§	Spirit (afrit, jinni) in the form of cat [no. 23]
F541.14.1.1§	‡"Eyelashes that would cover an acre" [see Afterword, n. 51]
F721.1.0.1§	‡Crystal (glass) tunnel [no. 3]
F771.1.4	‡Steel [(iron)] castle (house) [no. 12]
F819§	‡Sympathetic plant(s) [no. 26]
F913	Victims rescued from swallower's belly [no. 29]
F913.4§	Eagle with man in its belly fed much meat: too heavy to fly and victim is rescued [no. 11]
F952	Blindness miraculously cured [no. 13]
F1041.21.9.1§	Death from shame (humiliation) [no. 27]
F1045	Night spent in tree [no. 13]

G. Ogres [And Satan]

G61	Relative's flesh eaten unwittingly [no. 16]
G412.3§	‡Ogre's (ogress's) fire lures person [no. 17]
G412.4§	‡Person falls into ogre's (ogress's) power when he goes to the predator's dwelling seeking help (usually to borrow household article: fire, salt, sieve, etc.) [no. 1]
G443§,	Ogre adopts human child [no. 11]
G512.3	‡Ogre burned to death [no. 25]

H. Tests

H51	Recognition by scar [no. 8]
H51.1	Recognition by birthmark [no. 15]

H501.4§	‡Test of reaching puberty (physical development, i.e., maturation) [no. 4]
H1578	Test of sex [(gender)]: to discover person masking as of another sex [no. 8]

J. The Wise and the Foolish

J226.8§	‡Choice: to save a person or goods (e.g., son or cow, wife or her jewelry, etc.) [no. 17]
J758	Beware of following an interested adviser [no. 31.2]
J1111	Clever girl [no. 10]
J1117.4§	Hedgehog (porcupine) as trickster [nos. 19, 20]
J1129§	Female trickster [no. 10]
J1141.1.19.1§	‡Confession sought or obtained by torture [no. 4]
J1215§	‡Know-all person ("*Abu-el-'Urraif*"): a talkative fool [no. 31]
J1563.5	Guest frightened away by housewife [(host's wife)] [no. 21]
J1833.2§	‡Shooting (striking) at a pest (bird, insect) alighted on animal's horn (back): hitting animal [no. 31.1]
J2199	‡Absurd shortsightedness—miscellaneous [no. 31.4]
J2624	Fright at animals' eyes in the dark [no. 31–2]

K. Deceptions

K99.1.1§	Contest in commercial prowess won by deception [no. 10]
K231.1.1.2	Mutual agreement to divide [(share)] food. Trickster eats other's food and then refuses to divide his own [no. 13]
K235.2.2§	‡Bag of gold (silver) expected, but bag of scorpions (snakes) received [no. 28]
K289§	Artificial (deceptive) compliance: one party to a bargain arranges for the terms (conditions, stipulations) to occur [no. 4]
K477.0.1.1.1.1§	‡Angry person (animal) deprives household of use of fire by extinguishing its source (wetting matches or the like) [no. 1, 9]

K512	Compassionate executioner. A servant charged with killing the hero (heroine) arranges the escape of the latter [no. 8]
K741.1	Capture by tarring [(placing gum on)] back of horse [no. 12]
K778	Capture through the wiles of a woman [no. 5]
K1020	Deception into disastrous attempt to procure food [no. 19]
K1025.3§	‡Trickster pretends to produce strips of meat from own body: foolish imitator dies attempting to do the same [no. 19]
K1349.8.1§	‡Entrance into maiden's room through secret passage (tunnel, hole in wall, etc.) [no. 3]
K1523	Underground passage [(tunnel)] to paramour's house. (Inclusa) Woman goes from one to the other [no. 3]
K1823.0.4§	‡Disguise as animal (bird) so as to hunt (catch game: bird or animal) [no. 18]
K1941	Disguised flayer. An imposter dresses in the skin of his victim [no. 12]
K2116.1.1.1	Innocent woman accused of eating her new-born children [no. 15]
K2127	‡False accusation of theft [no. 26]
K2137.1§	"Both are yours, if you catch me!" The husband is made by his faithless wife to believe that his guest has fled with "both" geese, and guest that husband is after his testicles. A chase ensues: husband: "Give me one." Guest retorts [no. 21]
K2212.0.2	Treacherous sister as mistress of robber (giant) plots against brother [no. 2]
K2212.2.2§	‡Treacherous husband's sister: plots against her brother's wife (fiancée) [no. 2]
K2251.1	Treacherous slave-girl [no. 9]
K2284	Treacherous priest [(cleric, sheik, *mulla*)][no. 27]
K2400§	‡Deception for deception (tit for tat): deceived person gets even in a like manner (same ruse, strategy, trick, etc.) [no. 19]

L. Reversal of Fortune

L111.4.4	Mistreated orphan hero [no. 26]
L406§	Hunter (predator) becomes hunted (prey) [no. 18]
L432.2	Impoverished father begs from daughter he has banished: recognized [no. 22]

M. Ordaining the Future

M225	Eyes exchanged for food [no. 13]
M250.1§	‡Deathbed wish: dying person (father, mother, husband, wife, etc.) makes a wish [no. 4]
M341.2.19	Prophecy: death at hands of certain person [no. 1]

N. Chance and Fate

N102.1§	Woman (girl) luckless in spite of beauty, virtue, and wealth no. 24]
N120.2§	‡Name (word, statement, etc.) harbinger of evil [no. 30]
N134.0.1§	Person brings good luck [no. 30]
N331.1.5§	‡Object (rock, shoe, knife, projectile, etc.) thrown,causes unintentional killing [no. 31.1]
N331.1.5.2§	‡Object carried by flying bird (or airplane) drops and kills person (animal) [no. 1]
N338	Death as result of mistaken identity: wrong person killed [no. 18]
N365.3.3§	Boy finds a woman's hair and decides to marry the person to whom it belongs: it is his sister's [no. 5]
N888.1§	‡Helper belonging to adversary religious persuasion [no. 9]

P. Society

P200.0.1.2.1§	‡Father protects children against stepmother (his wife) [no. 4]
P200.0.2.1§	Father is powerless [see Afterword, n. 47]

P200.1.1§	Mother as head of single-parent family [no. 29]
P209.1§	Mother as provider [no. 29]
P250.0.1.3§	‡Brother and sister undergo similar experiences [no. 5]
P252.2	Three sisters [no. 3]
P253.0.1.2§	‡Brother(s) need(s) a sister (be born) [no. 6]
P253.0.2	‡One sister and two brothers [no. 5]
P253.1.1§	Brother as guardian of his sister's chastity (sexual-honor) [no. 8]
P253.1.1.1§	Brother is to execute his sister; he is compassionate: spares her life [no. 8]
P254.0.1§	‡Household composed of only brother and sister(s). They live alone in palace (house, cave, etc.) [no. 25]
P264.4§	Inherent rivalry between a man's sister and his future wife (fiancée, sweetheart, etc.) [no. 2]
P272	Foster mother [no. 26]
P272.0.1§	‡Treacherous foster mother [no. 26]
P426.0.8§	‡Immoral (corrupt) cleric [no. 27]
P426.2.1.2§	‡Person disappointed with social life becomes hermit (anchorite, ascetic, etc.) [no. 3]
P550.1§	‡War [no. 5]
P771.3§	‡Goods for services [no. 2]
P771.3.1§	‡Food for a service (e.g., ear of corn for a shave, egg for knife sharpening, and the like) [no. 16]
P788.1§	‡Excessive shame (dishonor, disgrace: 'ar, khizy) from violation of mores [no. 22]

Q. Rewards and Punishments

Q40	Kindness rewarded [no. 23]
Q242.7§	‡Brother's incestuous desire with +his sister punished [no. 5]
Q280	Unkindness punished [no. 23]
Q291.3§	‡Hard-hearted parent(s) punished [no. 22]
Q411.4	Death as punishment for treachery [no. 4]
Q414	Punishment: burning alive [no. 14]
Q416	Punishment: drawing asunder by horses [no. 15]
Q440.1§	‡Punishment: expulsion from family (person disowned, disinherited) [no. 22]

Q552.2.3.5§	‡Treacherous (guilty) person sinks into earth (swallowed by earth) [no. 14]
Q552.3.3	‡Drought as punishment [no. 5]

R. Captives and Fugitives

R135.1	Crumb (grain) trail eaten by birds [no. 25]
R153.3	Father rescues son(s) [no. 17]
R351.0.1§	Maiden in tree discovered by her reflection in water [no. 25]

S. Unnatural Cruelty

S11.1.2§	Cruel father exposes daughter(s) [no. 22]
S73.1	Fratricide [no. 31–1]
S110.0.2§	Suicide intended (attempted) [no. 26]
S117	‡Death by dragging behind horse [no. 15]
S301	Children abandoned (exposed) [no. 14]

T. Sex

T11.1	Love from mere mention or description [no. 3]
T52.10.1§	‡Girl will marry with a stipulation [no. 25]
T52.11.1§	Sister marries to save brother(s) [no. 25]
+T121.8.2§	‡Man (youth) of respectable social rank weds lowly girl (vagabond, beggar, etc.) [no. 14]
T115.2§	‡Woman (girl) marries ogre [no. 22]
T131.11.1§	Descent (ancestry) as obstacle to marriage [no. 14]
T160.0.3§	Publication of defloration: blood displayed [no. 27]
T205.1§	Wife-beating [no. 4]
T670.1§	‡Childless couple adopt child [no. 26]

U. The Nature of Life

U194.2§	‡Rumors spread quickly [no. 3]

W. Traits of Character

W171.0.2§	‡"To be of two intents: [a declared good one and a harbored evil (malicious) one]" (*Abu-niyyatain*) [no. 13]
W179.1§	‡Power of hatred (envy, jealousy, malice, etc.) [no. 3]
W181	Jealousy [no. 3]
W195.3§	Being loved (favored) within family envied [no. 3]
W195.9.3§	Sister envies sister's handsome husband (suitor, lover) [no. 3]

Z. Miscellaneous Groups of Motifs

Z71.5.1	Seven brothers and one sister [no. 1]
Z88§	‡Sarcasm [no. 27]
Z121.0.1.1§	‡Honest intentions personified (*"Niyyah Salimah"*) [no. 13]
Z127.0.3.1§	‡Dishonest intentions personified (*"Niyyah Su'"*) [no. 13]
Z292.0.1.1§	‡Tragic ending of a story (tale): all die [no. 1]

Suggested Readings

Tale Collections from Morocco

'Abd-al-'Al, 'Abd-al-Mun 'im S. *Lahjat shamal al-maghrib: Tutwan wa ma hawlaha* (The dialect of northern Morocco: Tetouan and its environs). Cairo, 1968.

Chimenti, Elisa. *Tales and Legends of Morocco*. Aaron Benami, trans. New York, 1965.

Colin, Georges Séraphin. *Recueil de Textes en Arabe Marocain*. Paris, 1937.

Destaing, Edmond. *Textes arabes en parler des Cheluhs du Sous (Maroc)*. Paris, 1937.

Duqaire, H. *Anthologie de la littérature marocaine*. Paris, 1937.

Dwyer, Daisy H. *Images and Self-Images, Male and Female in Morocco*. New York, 1978.

Laoust, Emile. *Contes berbères du Maroco*. 2 vols. Paris, 1949–50.

———. *Étude sur le dialecte berbèr du Chenoua*. Paris, 1912.

Légey, Françoise. *Contes et légendes populaires du Maroc, recueillis à Marrakech*. Paris, 1926.

Leguil, Alphonse, I. *Contes berbères du Grand Atlas*. Paris, 1985.

———. *Contes berbères de Atlas de Marrakech*. Paris, 1988.

Loubignac, Victorien. *Textes arabes des Zaërs*. Paris, 1952.

Noy, Dov, ed. *Moroccan Jewish Folktales*. New York, 1966.

Quinel, Charles, and A. de Montgon. *Contes et légendes du Maroc*. Paris, 1951.

Scelles-Millie, Jeanne. *Contes arabes du Maghreb*. Paris, 1970.

Shakir, Yusri. *Hikayat min al-folklore al-maghribi* (Tales from Maghribian folklore). 2 vols. Casablanca, [1978], 1985.

Socin, Albert. "Zum arabischen Dialekt von Marokko." In *Abhandlungen der philologisch-historischen Klasse der königlische Sächsischen Gessellschaft der Wissenschaften zu Leipzig*. Vol. 14. Leipzig, 1893, 149–203.

Stumme, Hans. *Märchen der Schluh von Tázerwalt*. Leipzig, 1895

Tale Collections from Various Maghreb Countries, Some of Which Contain Texts from Morocco

Amrouche, Marguerite Taos. *Le grain magique: contes, poemes et proverbes berbères de Kabylie*. Paris, 1966.

al-Baqluti, al-Nasir, ed. and trans. *Hikayat sha'biyyah min Tunis (Contes populaires de Tunisie)*. Sfax, 1988.

Basset, René. "Contes et légendes arabes." *RTP*, 18–19 (1903–14).

———. *Contes populaires berbères*. Paris, 1887.

———. *Nouveaux contes berbères*. Paris, 1897.

Belamri, Rabah. *La rose rouge* Paris, 1982.

Bouhdiba, 'A. *L'imaginaire maghrebin: tude de dix contes pour enfants*. Tunis, 1977.

Frobenius, Leo. *Volksmärchen der Kabylen, Atlantis*. Vols. 1–3. Jena, 1921–22.

Galley, Micheline. *Badr az-Zen et six contes algeriens*. Paris, 1971.

Houri-Pasotti, Myriam. *Contes de Ghazala*. Paris, 1980.

Lacoste, Camille, ed. *Légendes et contes merveilleux de la grande Kabylie*, recueillis par Auguste Mouliéras. Paris, 1965.

Lévi-Provençal, Evariste. *Textes arabes de l'Ouargha*. Paris, 1922.

Renaud, Jean, and Tahar Essafi, *La sorcière d'Emeraude*. Paris, 1929.

Reesink, Pietre. *Contes et Récits Maghrébin*. Québec, 1977.

sahykod/(S.A.H.Y.K.O.D.), *Lundja: Contes du Maghreb*. Paris, Harmattan, 1987.